I0672731

Brainstorm

Inspired by True Events
The Story of a Struggle against Insurmountable Odds

by

William Blackwell

Story Idea and Contributions by Donna Williams

BRAINSTORM

First edition. March 9, 2012.

ISBN: 978-1738971428

Written by William Blackwell.

"*Brainstorm* is a strong, compelling story of courage and personal transformation. Blackwell has obviously done a lot of research and invested his spirit in the characters as he tells the story of Garnet's harrowing medical condition through the three very different perspectives: Garnet's, his wife, and their friend, Ella. They are all unique and compelling characters and Blackwell builds strong character arcs for all three ... he does a fabulous job of making the reader care deeply about them and about what happens to them."

—Winslow Eliot

Acknowledgements

I would like to thank the following people:
The family who inspired the book. Their courage is amazing.
Winslow Eliot, for her words of encouragement and excellent editing.
Telemachus Press, for their professionalism and encouraging words.
Gwen, who helped me overcome my demons.
All my friends who supported my writing.

For those who toil without hope.

Brainstorm

Chapter One

The bed rocked back and forth violently as Garnet Dewitt clutched the mattress, his fingers turning white with the force of his grip. His eyes rolled, saliva dripping down the corner of his mouth. His entire body shook violently with the force of the seizure. He consciously stopped rolling his eyes and glanced around the room.

Cameras monitored his every move. Electrodes were plugged into his head and hooked to a computer screen that displayed brain activity. He also had a little hand control with a button that he was supposed to press at the onset of a seizure. But the seizures always seemed to take him by surprise, and he never had time to press it.

On the other side of the two-way glass in front of him, doctors watched, taking copious notes. It was late September 2010, and Garnet was in the newly opened seizure monitoring unit at Calgary Foothills Hospital. He was having an induced seizure, an attempt to confirm that he would make a good candidate for a temporal lobectomy, a brain surgery that would remove parts of his temporal lobe, including the hippocampus and amygdale. Doctors at the hospital suspected this scarred area of Garnet's brain was the source of his seizures.

This is strange, Garnet thought. *I'm actually enjoying myself. I never thought I would see the day when I would actually enjoy having a seizure.* Since he'd been in the hospital, now three weeks, doctors had taken him off the anti-seizure medication and had tried to create an environment to induce the epileptic seizures or, as Garnet liked to call them, "electrical storms in my brain."

So far, doctors had induced 35 seizures, and their analysis would try to determine whether the seizures stemmed from the temporal lobe area of Garnet's brain, which could then be operated on, or from multiple areas of the brain, in which case Garnet's epileptic condition would be rendered inoperable.

If that was the case, Garnet would then have to live his life, as he had up to this point, knowing that any little stress could trigger a violent electrical impulse storm in his head.

Garnet had had many such seizures up to this point. Some of them were petit mal seizures, where he stayed conscious but just went completely blank, or absent, for a few minutes. Others were psychomotor seizures, where he would go blank and behave in strange ways. Still others were of the grand mal type, which involved violent convulsions, unconsciousness, extreme soreness and muscle pain when they ended.

During many of Garnet's seizures, he would only remember waking up bruised and battered in an ambulance or in the hospital, after doctors had medically revived him. When he was younger, one grand mal seizure had been so violent it had lasted seven hours and Garnet had to spend a week in the hospital, recovering.

He had been taking anti-seizure medication for as long as he could remember. He found the medication didn't seem to help much with the seizures, but it certainly affected his cognitive functioning, slowing his speech considerably and dulling his senses to the point where he had difficulty processing information.

Almost like a scene from *The Exorcist*, Garnet and his bed continued to rock violently back and forth. The seizure was nearing the eight-minute mark and seemed to be building strength, like a Tsunami wave does before it crests and wreaks a violent swath of destruction.

A smile came over Garnet's face, and doctors on the other side of the two-way glass exchanged puzzled glances as they looked at the computer screen.

Why am I enjoying this so much? Garnet mused. He guessed it was because he was actually conscious of what was happening, and during many of his other seizures he had blacked out completely. Many of the other seizures in the outside world were probably triggered by stress, and the outcome of those seizures was always unsure. He could fall down, smack his head and die, as his epileptic aunt had done. He also reasoned, in his gyrating condition, that the stress-free and controlled environment he was in contributed to his enjoyment.

He fell short of breaking out into hysterical laughter before the seizure eventually subsided. He felt the bed's movement slow, and his vice-like grip on the mattress begin to loosen. He felt his body begin to relax, and he could feel the electrical impulses in his brain weaken. *I wonder if this is how it would feel to be electrocuted*, he mused, before a young blonde nurse with stunning blue eyes and a warm smile entered the room and snapped him out of his reverie.

"How are you feeling, Garnet? You seemed to be enjoying that experience." She walked to his bedside and began wiping the sweat from his brow with a clean towel.

He realized he was now slumped over in the bed. He processed her words, but it took him a few moments, as he still felt like his mind was in another zone, another reality of sorts.

"Uhhh ... I'm okay. It's the, the stress free environment, I guess ... makes it kinda' pleasant."

The nurse removed some of the straps constricting his legs and arms to the mattress. Garnet slumped to one side, soaked in sweat.

"Let's get you up here, young man," she said, gently positioning his head on the pillow. "I want you to rest right now, with no stimulus. Your dinner will be here in half an hour. Relax and then eat. Your neurologist, Daniel Carsdale, will be in later this week to talk to you. We still have a lot of data to analyze, but you may be a good candidate for surgery."

Garnet stared at Nurse Janice Priestly. His mind felt numb now, and the brief enjoyment had faded as he contemplated his situation. She left and he stared out the window. He listened to the wind whistling. Flakes of snow swirled and landed on his window, melting on contact. He suddenly felt cold.

What disturbed him was the surgery he may have to undergo. A very difficult and dangerous surgery it would be indeed.

Doctors had told him there was a 2% chance the surgery would cause a stroke, rendering him seizure-free, but potentially with severe brain damage. Even worse, severe brain damage and an inability to walk or have any basic motor functions in his extremities. Garnet wondered what was worse; being severely brain damaged with limited motor functions, or carrying on with constant electrical storms in his brain.

Then he remembered what one doctor had said to him and realized the surgery was his only option. About 20 years ago, Garnet had tried to get medical clearance to get his driver's license. After a short conversation, the doctor declared, "I am sorry to inform you, Mr. Dewitt, that you suffer from mild mental retardation. Let's face it, you will never graduate from any university." That comment had stayed with Garnet to this day. In fact, he wasn't sure if it would ever leave him.

Although he was not one to dwell on negativity, that statement had ripped Garnet's heart, and he remained determined to one day prove the good doctor wrong. Needless to say, the doctor did not give Garnet medical clearance to get a driver's license.

Doctors had also told him there was a small chance of dying and a small chance of continuing to have seizures after the surgery. Still, he didn't have a lot of options, as he saw it. And it could well be that even after the surgery, he would have to continue taking anti-seizure medication for the rest of his life.

Garnet liked his chances. After all, he had a wife and a 17-year-old daughter to support. And they needed him. Badly.

When Garnet had first laid eyes on Ella in 1986 at The Mustard Seed church, he said to himself, "This is the woman I am going to marry." And marry her he did, after a two-year courtship.

Ella, although very intelligent, was not a person others would consider normal. At a young age, she suffered brain damage, the result of a late diagnosis of a hyperthyroid gland. The brain damage left her with attention deficit disorder, weak short-term memory, and poor hand-eye coordination. By her own admission, she often tripped over her own feet and stumbled, righting herself moments before falling completely.

The brain damage also rendered her confused, and at times she was unable to process information quickly. She was also prone to emotional outbursts, and Garnet sometimes wondered if those outbursts were due to her frustration with her limitations. She could work all right, but her progress was slow, and this had proven to be a serious impediment to her becoming gainfully employed.

On the other hand, Ella had a certain intelligence and grasp of complicated concepts that most doctors would consider unusual, given her level of brain damage. Her mind drifted at times, and her eyes took on a glazed look, leaving many who met her with the impression that she was retarded.

But through this exterior she could, at times, grasp certain situations and conversations with a whip-like quickness and clarity. Her physical appearance belied her occasional astute wit and razor sharp intelligence. But the appearance of mental retardation had handicapped Ella in many ways.

We live in a physical world, and it is no surprise that attractiveness wins promotions, higher social status, and excellent careers. People who are born unattractive have to work harder to achieve their goals. And with Ella's physical and mental limitations, life was tough. She struggled to succeed in a society that in many ways equates appearance and material possessions with intelligence. So she went about her life, undaunted by the cultural and social norms. She worked many different jobs, but they didn't last long.

Chapter Two

Ella's latest job was a foray into selling investments with The World Financial Group. She had to write the preliminary exam six times before finally passing it on the seventh try. Undaunted, she was now preparing for the final exam—her second attempt at it. She sat in her run-down two-story townhouse in Rundle and contemplated her investment broker career. She had the practice questions in front of her, but was distracted.

Her mind drifted back to Garnet. She looked at her watch. It was 4:15 pm. Visiting hours were over at nine, and she planned on bringing her daughter Susan up to see Garnet within the next few hours. She couldn't call him, as the hospital did not allow cell phones, and they certainly didn't have the money to pay for a private hospital phone.

She tried to focus on preparation for the final exam. Suddenly her black cat Pickles leaped up on the kitchen table where she was working, gave her an inquisitive look, then dashed away as quickly as he had landed, sending papers and books flying in all directions. The papers floated slowly down and settled on the already-cluttered floor. Ella was a lot of things, but a good housekeeper she was not. Susan was watching TV when the action caught her attention and she burst out into laughter.

"Pickles, you silly cat," Ella, said, unable to drown out Susan's laughter. Pickles disappeared. Maybe he had a plan to reappear after things settled down. *I will never know*, she thought as she bent down and began methodically picking up the pieces of her life. By this time, Susan's giggles subsided and she returned to her show.

Ella tried to fix her mind on her homework. Suddenly she was hit by a brainstorm, although not the kind her husband currently suffered from.

She picked up the phone and dialed her realtor friend Debbie. She would try and sell her some insurance, she decided, and make some money so Garnet could have a private line at the hospital.

Chapter Three

Debbie Dupree was the epitome of a successful realtor. She had it all. Tall, statuesque brunette, a body with the curves in all the right places. She was beautiful, with stunning green eyes and soft, olive-toned skin.

She worked for ReMax Real Estate in southwest Calgary, in an office with about 165 other realtors. Debbie was consistently a top ten realtor in the office. She worked hard, was a tenacious negotiator, and could easily manage twenty-two listings and six buyers at the same time. This, with the help of two full-time assistants and a full-time chauffer, all at her beck and call.

If Ella had to analyze Debbie's life, and she often did, as they had been long-time friends, she would point to one thing that was missing.

Love.

After eight years of marriage, Ella was still passionately in love with Garnet. Debbie, on the other hand, after two failed marriages, remained single. But Ella was nevertheless amazed at Debbie's work ethic, her success, and her multi-tasking ability.

Ella remembered on one visit she had tried to count the number of tasks Debbie was doing simultaneously, and couldn't. Ella wondered if it was her brain damage that rendered her unable to count the tasks, or if there were simply too many to count.

"That's impossible," Ella said aloud to herself, and Susan looked up from her show.

Pickles had returned downstairs, and he seemed to be contemplating another attack on the insurance homework. He circled the kitchen table and eyed the papers with a predatory focus, only looking up momentarily at Ella's declaration. Pickles would not be denied his prey.

Ella suddenly realized the phone was ringing and she struggled to remember who she was calling. "Right, Debbie," she said. She also realized, with more than a little dissatisfaction, that her mind often worked that way.

Debbie sat at the captain's chair of what she liked to call Command Central, a well-organized system of offices prestigiously located in Lake Bonavista Estates. The offices were on the second floor of an upscale, five-million-dollar home perched on the shore of the city's first premiere lake community.

Four of the five rooms had lake views, and these had been converted to offices ten years ago when Debbie bought the property and had it renovated. She negotiated on the phone while she looked out at the lake, the sun illuminating her perfect complexion. She was 45-years-old, but could easily pass for 30.

"Okay, Rick, it's like this ... we've been going back and forth now for a few hours, and frankly my clients are getting a little tired of this nickel and diming." She instantly wondered if she had gone too far and might have pissed off the listing realtor.

But she was on a roll, and also had another negotiation in the works. She had thirty minutes to review a listing presentation and fly out the door. She wanted to wrap this deal up, a deal that would secure a property for $450K. In her estimation, the property was worth at least $500K. She had been tipped to the seller's motivation when, during a showing, a bill collector showed up at the door and mistook her client, a mild mannered accountant, for the owner, demanding repayment of a debt.

"Nickel and diming?" Rick Fowler cut in before Debbie could finish. "Your clients are trying to steal this property." Now he did sound a little pissed.

Debbie tried another tact. "Okay Rick, we both know the value of the property, that is not in dispute here. But my clients have a number in their minds, regardless of how many comparable solds they look at, that they're willing to pay. Unfortunately, my friend, that number is 450, max. If your clients are not willing to take it, we will let the offer expire, which it will in an hour, as you know, and we will move on. Simple as that. This is a take it or leave it counter. I have brought my people up from 425, and I am afraid that is the very best I can do." Debbie thought her inside knowledge of the client's financial distress would prevail in this deal, and it would indeed close.

"I'll pass it on to my clients and call you back," Fowler said, and abruptly hung up the phone before Debbie could get another word in. She had noticed while she was talking to Fowler that one of her secretaries was standing in front of her with a telephone, but knew better than to interrupt Debbie during a negotiation.

"Your friend is on the phone," Lisa announced after Debbie hung up.

Debbie smiled. "Oh, who might that be?"

"Ella. Your favourite person."

Debbie grimaced slightly. As much as she tired of Ella and what she viewed as her delusions of grandeur, she was her friend, and she would talk to her. Debbie knew something about success. She hadn't gotten to where she was now by ignoring people, even people she didn't necessarily like.

In this business, she thought, *you never know where your next deal will come from.*

Debbie took a deep breath, watched a bird soar past her window and begin its flight over the lake in the afternoon glistening sun, forced a smile to her lips, and clicked the line on her desk that was Ella.

"Ella, Ella, How are you, my dear? So funny that you called as I was just thinking about you." Although this wasn't true, Debbie knew that it would please Ella greatly.

"Garnet is in the hospital. They might have to do brain surgery."

"Oh, that's awful news," Debbie said. "Is there anything I can do?"

"Well, umm ... I am studying to become an insurance salesperson, and I was wondering if you would like to buy some insurance," Ella said.

"But how can you sell insurance if you haven't ..." Debbie's other line started beeping and she could see it was Fowler on the line. "Excuse me, dear, could you hold for just a minute? I really have to take this call." Before Ella could answer, Debbie clicked the hold button and immediately had Fowler on the line.

"So where are we at, my friend?" she said, knowing that a call back this quickly likely meant good news.

"It's a done deal," Fowler said.

"Excellent," Debbie said, motioning for her secretary to take the call and sort out the final initials and signing of the contract. "Here's Lisa to sort out the details. Pleasure doing business with you."

Without missing a beat, Debbie removed Ella from her hold position and put her on the speakerphone, motioning to her secretary at the same time to close the door on her way out.

"If you haven't finished the course, how can you sell insurance?" Debbie asked.

"My boss said I can do it under his name until I graduate. And Garnet needs a phone in his room so I can keep in touch with him, make sure he's okay."

"I really hate to rain on your parade, Ella, but I do not think selling insurance is your thing, and I do not believe you will even complete the course. So, no, I'm sorry, but I don't want to buy insurance."

Ella seemed disheartened, but Debbie masterfully steered the conversation away from the insurance and toward Garnet and his condition. After promising to visit Garnet in the hospital, she said goodbye and went back to her second negotiation. She had about five minutes to close the deal before reviewing the numbers on a property evaluation Lisa was in the middle of preparing.

She anticipated the phone would ring at any moment. And she hadn't gotten to this pinnacle of success by being wrong on her hunches.

Debbie's other negotiation involved some investors on a property in Acadia. A middle class neighbourhood, Acadia consisted of 1960's homes, some multi-family apartments and at least a few run-down duplex-style rentals. It was a centrally located transitional area occupied by original owners who were nearly dead, as well as much younger families who were replacing the older folk. The area was also popular with house flippers and investors seeking long-term, stable rental revenue.

Debbie, on behalf of her clients, had submitted an offer of $315,000. They were trying to buy a 1057-square-foot, three-bedroom bungalow in original condition with a developed basement, two full baths, in a great location, with a nice yard, mature trees, and a single detached garage. In her gut, she knew that home in today's real estate market was worth at least $345,000. It had been under listed at $325,000. She had met her clients at the property the first day it was listed, as the software realtors now used would automatically send new listings to clients. In many cases, the clients would receive the emails before their realtors did.

Debbie was also on the cutting edge of technology and all her emails went right into her smartphone as well as the inbox of her computer. She didn't miss a beat.

Like clockwork, the phone rang. She looked at the number. It was Bill Mizner, the listing realtor.

"Hello, Bill," she said sweetly. "I hope you have something I can work with."

"Actually, this news isn't so good," Mizner said. "I am afraid we have two more offers coming in."

Shit, Debbie thought. She quickly told Mizner she would advise her clients and get back to him.

Debbie knew the protocol with respect to multiple offers on Alberta real estate. Although one or more of the real estate boards periodically made changes to this protocol, probably just to confuse realtors and create material for more education courses, Debbie knew that currently, multiple offers meant a bidding war.

Debbie's clients, in light of this new information, now had essentially three choices: withdraw their offer, leave it and let the chips fall where they may, or adjust the price and possibly the conditions. Debbie knew her clients well, and felt they were the type of people not to go a penny over list price, in spite of the fact the property was worth more than their offer.

Based on a line of credit financing at 20% down, the property also showed a modest $350 monthly positive cash flow after expenses (if it was rented out), even if her clients paid full list.

It made sense to even go over list-based on the numbers, but Debbie believed this would be against her clients' better judgement. No matter the value, some people inherently have a problem paying over list price for real estate.

She worked out her strategy. Suggest full list price, and diplomatically suggest removal of home inspection and finance conditions. Debbie knew the mortgage broker well, and he had assured her financing was guaranteed. Her clients' financial situation and credit score were outstanding. Although realtors are not allowed to advise clients not to have a home inspection on a property, they can certainly inform them that if the home inspection condition is removed, they would have a much better chance of buying it.

And it has to be worded ever so cleverly in order to avoid getting my ass sued off, Debbie thought.

Five minutes on the phone, and she had a no-condition offer coming through her fax at full list price.

Five minutes after that, she received a call from Mizner saying congratulations.

Her clients were elated. Debbie rose from her captain's chair, grabbed her black suit jacket, picked up the property evaluation, and motioned for Lisa to have the chauffer meet her at the front door of her palatial home.

The second negotiation had taken about ten minutes longer than Debbie had anticipated, and she would have to wing it on the listing presentation. Don pulled up in the black Lexus and screeched to a stop, knowing they were running a little late and he would have to make up some time.

In the back seat, Debbie talked to a new client on the phone and simultaneously reviewed the property evaluation for her listing presentation—a six million dollar estate style home in Mount Royal, one of the oldest and most prestigious upscale neighbourhoods in the city.

"Step on it," she said to Don. He glanced back with his toothy grin, put pedal to metal, and peeled out of the driveway.

Chapter Four

The next afternoon, Ella waited with her daughter at a bus stop a short distance from her Rundle townhouse.

It was plus ten Celsius, not particularly warm for that time of the year. Ella did not complain, however. She merely looked around at the patchwork assortment of run-down apartments in her neighbourhood, many with garbage, old cars, and kids toys littering lawns and curbsides. Some units were occupied by single mothers or disenfranchised couples who engaged in all night, knock-down, drag-out fights after abusing one or more different drugs. She also knew there were a couple of crack houses just down the block. If you had nothing better to do, you could watch the action unfold close to your front doorstep. Hookers and junkies came and went, and occasionally an argument would erupt when a customer felt cheated on price or quality. Sometimes the addicts would argue for no apparent reason.

Ella also knew the house at the end of the block was reportedly occupied by organized crime gangs.

"Mom, do you think we'll ever end up in a better neighbourhood?" Susan asked, seeming to sense her mother's thoughts. Susan had long black hair, inquisitive eyes and a warm smile. The gods had been kind to her facial features and they were easy to look at. She was developing into a perfectly normal young woman.

Ella hesitated, as she sometimes had trouble beginning sentences. "Umm ... yes, sweetie ... one day we will ... I'm sure of it."

Two teenaged girls were waiting at the bus stop a few feet away. One of them, with bright red hair, glanced over at Ella. "I think she's retarded," she said to her friend, gesturing indiscreetly toward Ella.

Her black-haired friend cackled. "She looks retarded."

"Creature from the black lagoon coming to get you," Red-head said, mock-strangling her friend.

"Get out of here," Black-head said, pushing her friend's hands away. "They shouldn't let people like that out in public. Don't we have nuthouses for freaks like her?"

Susan glared at the two girls, and was about to say something when Ella grabbed her hand.

The bus pulled up. Ella waited for the two girls to get on, let all the other passengers get in line, and took her place at the end of the line. She pulled a tissue from her pocket and dabbed at a few tears that were running down her cheeks. Susan hugged her and kissed her cheek.

Ella had to remind herself to stay positive for her visit with Garnet, but she had to admit the girls' comments had cut deeply. But she would not give the two little tramps the satisfaction of seeing her cry.

Memories of her childhood flooded back. She remembered being ignored, and worse, verbally abused by other students in school. She remembered chasing her so-called friends down the street, and them running away from her, encouraged by other kids not to hang around with her.

Ella could not remember a single friend she'd had in elementary or high school as she boarded the bus, deposited the fare, and searched for a seat far away from Red-head and Black-head. There was standing room only, but a kindly old man at the front of the bus stood up and offered Ella his seat. Susan stood as well.

Ella thanked the man. It made her feel better to realize that humankind was indeed capable of unconditional acts of kindness. She tried not to look at the two girls, sitting at the back of the bus, who were snickering and occasionally bursting into fits of laughter.

I've been discriminated against my whole life because I look mentally handicapped, Ella thought. *But I can't control what other people think, and never will, so best put it out of my mind.* She remembered reading somewhere that other people did not make you feel sad or happy; it was your own perception that governed your emotions. Ella tried to put a positive spin on this humiliating experience.

If karma indeed plays a role in our lives, those two will get their comeuppance, she decided.

Chapter Five

Garnet Andrew Dewitt was born in Halifax, Nova Scotia on August 22, 1962, to parents Lena and James. He was an only child. His mother was from Finland and worked as a nursing assistant. Garnet's father, originally from New Brunswick, was a drummer in a pipe and drum band for a while before starting his own business as a commercial artist. The two met while James was in the hospital, recovering from a fall.

Garnet's memories of his childhood were bittersweet. His father once told him, "If you put your brain into a bird, it would fly backwards." Needless to say, he wasn't particularly close to his father. He had a much stronger bond with his mother. He loved her dearly.

As Garnet grew up, he began to realize his parents' relationship was not all that harmonious. He noticed at age fifteen that his parents squabbled frequently, at times keeping him up at nights. They had also separated a few times for short durations as a result of these arguments.

When Garnet was sixteen years old, his father died of a heart attack. He had left for work in the morning after telling Garnet he would never amount to anything. Garnet had received a phone call that afternoon telling him his father had dropped dead at work. By that time, James had become obese, and he drank and smoked constantly.

Two years after his father's death, his mother was diagnosed with stomach cancer. Surgeons removed two thirds of her stomach before discovering that the cancer had spread to her liver and other vital organs. She died soon after.

Grief-stricken, Garnet sank into a deep depression that lasted about six months. On her deathbed, his mother arranged for Garnet to go into a group home. He was grateful that she had made sure he would be taken care of after she passed away. Garnet's parents were both in their early 50s when they died.

He thought of his parents now as he gazed out the window at the snow coming down, blowing into the windowpane and melting away quickly. He watched a bird crash into the window. It hovered, momentarily stunned, and then flew away. It reminded him of his father's comment, and he tried to push it out of his mind.

He had had another induced seizure that afternoon and now he was waiting for his dinner—a five-star hotel delicacy, he imagined, grinning in spite of his pain. The last seizure had lasted sixteen minutes, a long time by anyone's standard.

It was so violent he was able to rip away one of his wrist restraints with his right hand and began punching himself in the nose, the eye, and then the mouth. Now he was sporting a few cuts and bruises, the result of the superhuman strength epileptics often displayed during seizures. His muscles felt sore after being in a clenched and convulsive state for so long.

During the last seizure, he had noticed the violent "brainstorm" in his head had reached monumental proportion. He felt like a little man in the middle of a blinding, ferocious blizzard, and in his mind's eye he could see himself being swept away by the storm, his body wracked by hot and cold flashes. He also remembered an image of defeat, as if this fight had become too epic for him and perhaps it was easier just to acquiesce to its destructive force. That was when he felt three hard blows to his head, and he wondered if he had subconsciously tired of himself and tired of the battle; hence the self-inflicted war wounds.

Another thing bothered him. His head pounded with pain, and he suspected it wasn't only due to the headshots. When his right arm ripped through the leather strap binding him to the bed, Janice and Dr. Carsdale had rushed into the room, along with two porters, and physically restrained him. He remembered when he came out of the seizure, he had quite a few hands tightly gripping him to the bed, and their faces indicated physical stress.

Carsdale was sweating profusely and Janice was flushed red, the color starting from her face and spreading down to encompass her entire neck. She was very attractive, even in red, Garnet decided. It was one of her colors.

He did not remember having other seizures of that magnitude, and it worried him. He could not even see straight it was so powerful. The doctors had given him some Tylenol, but it had only dulled the pain slightly.

He might ask for something stronger, he decided. If he could remember.

The door opened and Janice walked in with a tray of food. She had evidently intercepted Food Services and decided to deliver it personally. Her clear eyes fixed on Garnet. "Hey sport, how are you doing? Here, I think it's better if you eat something to try and get some of your energy back."

She wheeled the tray over to Garnet's bed and watched him look at it. His head was throbbing, and he no longer had an appetite.

He noticed the redness on Janice's face again, except now it was just her cheeks and a few splotches on her neck.

"Okay," Garnet said, looking at the mush in front of him, trying to work up an appetite. He decided it wasn't a gourmet meal after all. "Is Dr. Carsdale coming in to see me today?"

"I believe he is, my dear. Now I will leave you to your food. Enjoy." The door closed behind her.

As Garnet picked at his food, the door opened and Ella and Susan, wet from the snow, walked in.

Garnet looked at Ella and smiled, although he knew the smile was half a grimace due to the pain and the welts on his face from his earlier round one victory over himself.

Ella's black hair was wet and dishevelled from the snow and wind. She was 50 but looked much older, the turmoil of her life showing on the cracks in her face. She smiled back at her husband and took three steps before tripping over one of her pigeon toes and stumbling to his bedside.

What a sight for sore eyes, Garnet thought as he kissed his wife and gave Susan a peck on the cheek.

"Uh ... what happened to your face, honey?" she asked as she leaned back from the embrace to take a good look at her husband.

His face still smarted from the wounds, but he tried another grin and declared, "I got into a mixed martial arts fight with myself, for a shot at the title. I won, honey. TKO referee stoppage in round one."

"Oh ... quit your teasing, Garnet." Ella couldn't help smiling. Susan found his remark hysterical, and burst into laughter. Soon, they were all laughing.

They were interrupted by Dr. Carsdale's entrance. The young doctor was about six feet tall, with short brown hair and large, black-rimmed spectacles that gave him an intellectual demeanour. Carsdale cared about his patients deeply, and it showed in his bedside manner.

"Hello, Garnet," he said, acknowledging Susan and Ella with a friendly nod. "We need to talk about a few things if you have some time. Or would you rather finish the visit with your family? I can come back later."

"No, no," Garnet said. "Let's have this discussion right now. I think it's better that my wife is here so she can find out what's going to happen to me. She worries a lot."

Carsdale pulled up a chair, sat, and opened the chart in his hand. "I am going to say some things you may already know, but I think it's important to recap your condition so you can get a better sense of what is going to happen here." Carsdale looked at the three of them. Garnet winced and motioned for him to proceed.

According to Carsdale, the latest EEG results (a reading of the electrical activity in the brain) had pinpointed that Garnet's epilepsy was localized. In fact, it showed that the source of the seizures was scar tissue in Garnet's temporal lobe and deep within the temporal lobe, the hippocampus and amygdale were also responsible for the seizures.

To correct the problem, Carsdale explained, Garnet would have to undergo resective surgery, a temporal lobectomy. Surgeons would cut into the side of his head, open a window, then go in and cut out the hippocampus, amygdale, and a portion of his temporal lobe. In 95% of these surgeries, patients showed a dramatic reduction in the number of seizures, and in some cases the seizures stopped altogether.

The temporal lobectomy, one of the most common types of epileptic surgeries, did not come without risks. Apparently, there was a 2% chance that Garnet would have a stroke during or after surgery, potentially rendering him seizure-free, but brain-damaged in other unknown ways. There was also a small chance that complications could result in death.

"While we're pretty sure the seizures are localized, we need to be one hundred percent sure. So we'll spend the next month analyzing the data and, if I'm right, we'll proceed with the surgery. I would like to keep you in the hospital for that month, if possible, to keep a close eye on your health."

Ella looked rattled and Susan frowned in concern.

"If the seizures are related to this scar tissue, and you've isolated it to the temporal lobe, won't there be scar tissue left over from the operation that could potentially create more seizures?" Garnet asked.

"That possibility is small," Carsdale said. "After we cut out a sizable part of one temporal lobe, the bone is replaced and secured back to the skull, and the scalp is sutured. That missing piece of the brain will then fill up with the fluid that lines your brain. The remaining scar tissue is clean scar tissue, unlike the scar tissue you would have after cutting yourself, for example. This clean, surgical scar tissue almost never causes irritation to the brain."

Carsdale also explained how, after the operation, it was not uncommon to experience headaches and nausea. Garnet would be given medication for this, along with anti-seizure medication. He would likely be in intensive care for a week or two after the operation. He added that patients who undergo this type of surgery generally return to work within one to three months, but may have to continue taking anti-seizure medication for the rest of their lives.

Garnet reflected on the possibility of returning to his piano teaching. It was his hope to one day develop his music career; he had quite a talent for piano, tuba, trombone and bass trombone.

He also hoped that someday Ella would be able to face her demons and the society that shunned her, and land a decent-paying job. As it was now, they were both unemployed, and their meagre savings would soon dry up. He feared they would soon lose their house.

It would not be the first time they had to stay with friends. They might have enough money for another month's rent and groceries. If it wasn't for the free government health care, they would be out on the street now.

He searched for the upside, as he often did. Better to be sick here than some third world country, or even the United States, where his medical bills would have racked up significantly by now. That thought comforted Garnet, and the thudding pain in his head finally began to subside.

He looked at his meal and shovelled a spoonful of mashed potatoes and gravy into his mouth. A large blob of it landed on Ella's jeans. She was so engrossed in what Carsdale was saying she didn't notice. She absently wiped her jeans, rubbing the mashed potato and gravy mixture into them, creating a light brown stain. She remained oblivious as Susan noticed the stain and smiled.

Carsdale continued, "There will be no more induced seizures. Some of the more recent ones have definitely taken a toll on you, and for some reason we have noticed the electrical neuron activity in the seizures of late has been a lot more powerful than previously induced seizures. In fact, your last seizure, a grand mal, was the largest we have recorded so far.

"As you know, epilepsy is a brain disorder that involves repeated, spontaneous seizures of many types. These seizures, caused by abnormally excited electrical signals in the brain, are incidents of disturbed brain function that can cause changes in attention, behaviour, and even death, in rare cases. If your wife had not rescued you from your recent psycho motor seizure, when you tried to venture outside in minus twenty degree weather with no coat on ... well, who knows what would have happened to you?" It was a rhetorical question. He continued. "We have monitored your situation for many years now, and over the years my concern for your health has increased exponentially. The effects of the medication you have taken your whole life are minimal at best. If the data comes back one hundred percent conclusive, then after surgery your chances of leading a productive, normal life are very good. Your seizures, which started off mild, have definitely intensified in ferocity and duration. The grand mal, or tonic-clonic seizure, as it is now known, is a type of seizure that affects the entire brain, as opposed to a more localized seizure. The grand mal is the one associated with violent convulsions, exactly the convulsions you've been having here lately.

"These grand mal seizures seem to have originated from your temporal lobe, as well as the petit mal and psychomotor seizures. However, as I said, we need to be one hundred percent sure, so the analyzing and monitoring stage will now begin."

Garnet picked at his half-eaten dinner as he listened. He was tired now and wanted to sleep.

Carsdale seemed to sense his fatigue and patted Garnet on the back. He nodded to Susan and Ella. "I am going to let you get some rest right now, Garnet," he said, hoping Ella and Susan would also take the hint and let Garnet sleep. "I'm sure you have more questions, but we can talk later."

Ella watched Carsdale leave, smearing another potato stain into her jeans as she did. Susan smiled. Garnet finally noticed what his wife was doing, picked up his napkin, grabbed her hand, and gently wiped it clean. She gawked at the stain on her jeans and Susan giggled. After some small talk about the progress of Ella's studies, Garnet kissed his wife, gave Susan a warm hug, and they left.

Ella and Susan walked down the corridor of the epilepsy unit. Ella eyeballed the long, brownish stain on her right pant leg. *It could almost pass for a shit stain,* she thought, and continued her journey home, stumbling every ten or twelve steps.

After they left, Garnet eyed his meal. Some potato droppings had landed on the sheets, and he wiped them away with his napkin, pushing the tray to the end of the bed so he could rest. He had, what seemed to him, a very short recovery time from the seizures before potentially going under the knife. Before his mind could take off in many different directions, Garnet drifted off into a deep sleep.

Chapter Six

It was the summer of 1979, and Garnet had just left Ernest Manning High School. He would have to take three buses to get home, and he was waiting for his first one when he suddenly felt dizzy. He grabbed the bus stop sign to steady himself. He felt a petit mal seizure coming on. His eyes glazed over, blankness enveloping him, and the seizure took hold.

The bus pulled up. Garnet fought to clear his head, trying to will this seizure to go away, but it seemed to have a different intention. He dropped the fare and staggered down the aisle. The seizure's intensity increased as he sat on the bus, and through his blurred vision he could hardly process where he was and what he was doing. Somehow, he managed to get off the bus downtown, his second stop before continuing to Marlborough. Some kids laughed at him as he staggered off the bus.

"Look at that freak," one teenage boy said to his friend, pointing at Garnet, and they began laughing. Garnet frowned and stepped off the bus, vomiting on the sidewalk immediately afterwards. He steadied himself again on the bus stop pole, knowing the worst was yet to come. For Garnet, vomiting was usually the precursor to a grand mal seizure.

He managed to stay conscious long enough to reach his second stop in Marlborough, where he had one more bus to board before arriving home. He stood at the last bus stop and wondered if he would make it. Then the electrical impulses in his brain reached cataclysmic proportion and he felt his body convulsing. He knew a grand mal was coming. He fell to the ground, convulsing, and felt the blackness take hold, rendering him unconscious.

"Garnet, Garnet, wake up," Janice said as she gently pushed his shoulder.

Garnet's eyes opened. He was disoriented. He thought he was waking up from the seizure and it was his mother standing over him, as it had been on that summer day in 1979, when he had regained consciousness in the hospital. "Mom ... mom," he said.

"Garnet, it's Janice. You were having a nightmare."

His eyes cleared. "Oh," he said, realizing where he was.

Janice reached for a fresh towel and wiped Garnet's brow, which was soaked in sweat. "Are you okay?" she asked.

"I'm fine," he said, after some hesitation.

After she left, Garnet thought about his seizures. He knew he had had a lot of them, but could only remember a few, as the mind-numbing medication prevented him from recollecting some of the events of his life.

He did remember his first seizure, at the tender age of six. He fell and smacked his head on the coffee table. When he woke, he was on the couch in his mother's arms.

And there would be many more to follow.

Garnet shuddered. He prayed for the day he would be seizure-free.

"Garnet, how are you?" The door burst open and in walked Debbie, making good on her promise to visit. Dressed impeccably in a black business suit, carrying an assortment of cut flowers, she looked stunning.

Garnet smiled. "How ... how are you?" Debbie placed the flowers on an end table and sat down beside Garnet's bed.

"They're ... beautiful," Garnet said slowly. "Thank you."

Garnet told Debbie of his recent induced seizures and how it looked like he would be a candidate for surgery. He talked slowly, as his head was still clearing from the recent nightmare. Debbie nodded at all the appropriate times, but it seemed to Garnet her mind was far away.

Debbie had first met the Dewitt family back in 2001. At that time, they owned a house in Martindale they wanted Debbie to sell.

She was finishing up the property evaluation, wondering if this couple was even mentally competent to legally sign a contract. She also wondered if it was the right thing for them to sell the house, but quickly pushed that thought from her mind. She eventually sold the house, realizing they were in dire financial straits.

"Are you ... are you okay?" Garnet asked.

"Oh, I'm fine, Garnet," she said.

Lately Debbie had been analyzing her life, looking at all her material possessions, her business successes, and wondering if it was all worth it. Seeing Garnet now, his meagre possessions, indomitable spirit, and positive attitude, made her feel inexplicably empty.

What do all these successes mean? she wondered as Garnet looked at her with concern. She had thought the visit to the hospital would make her feel better, but all it did was make her feel like her lifetime of material pursuits was in vain. *How could he be so positive and happy, given his current situation?* she wondered.

She stood up. "I'm totally great," she said with a smile. "Listen, you take care of yourself. I'll be in touch."

As she walked down the hall, her mind cleared and she looked at her cell phone, wondering when she could turn it back on.

Don pulled up just as she walked to the curb. He opened the door for her and they headed to Shepard, a small rural community recently annexed by the city, where she was supposed to meet Adam for his possession. She had a large food basket and a half a dozen bottles of expensive red wine, a housewarming gift for Adam and his wife Sharon.

Her phone rang. It was June, the listing realtor. "Keys are releasable on Shepard."

"Great," Debbie said, thanking her. She began to perk up. A payday would be coming soon. In a week, she would get her $9000 commission cheque deposited directly in her account.

She arrived at the house and greeted Adam. They completed a walk-thru of the property. The 1555-foot two-storey had been left clean and tidy, carpets shampooed, and all the unattached goods were in the property, as per the contract.

After a quick inspection of the garage, Debbie guided Adam into the double detached garage with his pick-up truck, where he would deposit the first load of possessions in what would be a full day of moving.

"Again, Adam, I want to thank you for giving me the opportunity to help you. And congratulations on the purchase of your new home. If there isn't anything else, then I'll leave you to it. Call me if you need anything."

Chapter Seven

Garnet looked across the room at Ella and momentarily wondered where he was. Ella smiled at him and walked over with a glass of pasty liquid. She set it on the table before him. He picked it up and drained it in three large gulps.

"Not so fast," Ella said. "You'll choke on it."

Ten-year-old Susan pushed around a toy Tonka truck on a cluttered floor. She looked up at her mother and started laughing.

Garnet and Ella were three days into a health fast, the third day of which allowed for a fruit shake with milk and protein powder.

Garnet felt weak from the previous day's fasting. Suddenly, his eyes went blank for a few moments, then re-focused on his wife. Ella knew enough to realize he had just had a petit mal seizure, and a worried expression darkened her features.

"Maybe this health thing isn't such a good idea," she said.

"I'll be fine," Garnet said, ever the optimist.

But while he dressed and prepared for that night's orchestra rehearsal, he felt himself blanking out repeatedly in a series of petit mal seizures.

By the time he arrived at church, he had blanked out several times, and it seemed to him one of the seizures may have been of the psychomotor variety, which often culminated in a violent grand mal seizure.

"Ready to go?" Mike, his music teacher and friend, said as they sat on stage and picked up their instruments.

Garnet's eyes were glazed over. He did not respond to Mike.

"Hey, buddy," Mike said, patting Garnet lightly on the shoulder. "You okay?"

Garnet's gaze flickered and came into focus. "I ... I'll be fine."

Mike looked at him, worried.

The conductor gave the signal and the orchestra started playing.

Garnet blew into the tuba and it thundered its bass sound, in harmony with the rest of the instruments. He felt his head clear momentarily, and then he went completely blank. He stood up, tuba in hand, and began convulsing on the stage. He teetered precariously close the edge, nearly falling off.

Mike dropped his trombone, yelling, "Someone call 911!"

Mike knew that epileptics could develop superhuman strength during seizures, and it was not advisable to get in the way. But concern for his friend overrode any concern for his own safety. He noticed Garnet's vice-like grip on the tuba, and tried to pry it from his hands.

In his convulsing state, Garnet swirled like a ballerina, whacking Mike across the head with the tuba and sending him careening into a seated group of surprised flutists.

Garnet moaned softly as he continued gyrating.

Mike got up, wiped a trickle of blood from a small cut above his right eyebrow, and came again toward Garnet. By this time, four or five of the other musicians were with him, and they approached with caution.

"I'll grab him by the back, and the rest of you go around front," Mike said quickly, and leaped up on Garnet's back. The four others moved in from the front and tackled Garnet, football style, knocking him down. He landed on his back, Mike sandwiched underneath. By this time, Garnet's convulsing had intensified, and his muscles and legs were beginning to stiffen. The moaning sound continued as the group tried to pry the tuba from his hands.

By this time, Mike had freed himself from the weight of Garnet's body, and was also attempting to release the tuba from Garnet's grip. In spite of their efforts, they could not pry it free.

Garnet's convulsions stopped and he froze like a rock, clutching the tuba, his fingers now white.

The ambulance arrived, and the paramedics loaded Garnet into the ambulance. He still gripped the tuba. In the ambulance, they revived him with a medical injection.

Garnet slept in the hospital bed, his hands gripping the tuba in a playing position. Mike stood beside him, worried.

"Wake up, Garnet," he said, shaking his shoulder. "You're dreaming."

Garnet's eyes opened and he stared at Mike. "Where's my tuba?" he asked, wiping his eyes and looking around the room. His forehead was beaded with perspiration.

Garnet wiped his glistening brow. Slowly, his situation came back to him.

"Mike ... how you doin'? Nice of you to come."

They began to talk about Garnet's music. Up to that point, he had reached the Royal Conservatory of Music's (RCM) level four for tuba and level two for bass trombone. He was also a self-taught trombone player.

Since one of Garnet's goals was to become a music composer, one of the courses Mike was helping him with was advanced rudiments, something any composer needs to master in order to put his ideas on paper. Garnet had failed his first attempt, as he took too much time on the questions and was not able to complete the exam. He felt the mind-numbing anti-seizure medication was his biggest barrier.

He had also studied piano from a young age and reached the RCM level nine, one level below that of a concert pianist. Prior to his hospitalization, Garnet had memorized all five pieces of music he would need to perform in order to achieve level ten. But, just before the exam, he suffered searing pain in his arms and hands and was not able to take the test. Although he had been diagnosed with Scoliosis (an incorrect curvature of the spine), Mike felt that it was Garnet's improper posture that had caused the pain.

And he told him as much. "I don't think it's the Scoliosis," he said. "You need to sit like this." He positioned himself in his chair with his back straight. "Not like this." He slumped forward in the chair. "That's how you do it."

"Okay," Garnet said. "I still have the pieces memorized. And, since I've been here, the pain in my arms has gone down quite a bit. I'll do my advanced rudiments over again, and go for the level ten once I get out of here."

Chapter Eight

Debbie and Ella sat together on a bench in Glenmore Park, overlooking the Glenmore reservoir. It was mid-afternoon and the sun was starting to take the morning chill out of the air. White clouds dotted the bright blue sky. The reservoir was still frozen over for the most part, save for a large puddle in the middle.

Ella had called Debbie about six times, and finally Debbie had decided to take time out to meet with her friend, although her busy schedule would probably only grant her a half hour at the most. In the parking lot behind them, Don paced around the Lexus, awaiting Debbie's signal to leave.

Debbie had a hunch what this meeting was about, but she couldn't be sure. And Ella would not tip her hand over the phone.

Ella rubbed her knee as they sat, and began flexing it. She was doing what she called "the chicken leg thing," trying to work out the soreness caused by the arthritis she suffered in her knees. At times the pain was so bad it forced her to walk with a limp.

Debbie was thinking about her next listing presentation. She had to evaluate a newer bungalow in Monteray Park. It had three bedrooms, a two-bedroom illegal basement suite (meaning that the zoning and the year of its construction did not comply with city bylaws), and a double detached garage. Lisa had pulled up the title and some comparable solds and it hadn't taken Debbie long to realize the owner was in upside down. The title showed the property had a $360,000 mortgage on it, and although she had not yet viewed it, Debbie figured the maximum value at about $340,000. She was thinking about how to delicately position this to the seller when Ella began speaking.

Ella told Debbie what it was like being ignored and looked down on by people because of the way she looked. "It was bad enough when I was in high school, people ignoring me and calling me names. I still get it, though. People assume this is the way I am, and I haven't got anything to offer."

"You have lots to offer, sweetie," Debbie said, her tone condescending. It seemed to Ella that Debbie's mind was on other things.

"They just don't think I can do a lot," Ella continued. "A whole lot of them are really arrogant people. I'd rather not be around them anyway."

Debbie looked at Ella and thought, not for the first time, that she was mentally tough.

"Just ignore them," Debbie said, wondering if she would lump herself in the arrogant category.

Debbie suspected Ella had another reason for wanting to meet, other than just to vent. She also knew that in spite of Ella's limitations, she was certainly not one to dwell on them. Sure, she would mention them to get them off her chest; she had to tell someone and probably did not want to burden her husband, especially in his condition. So she told Debbie. Debbie had heard it before, but usually Ella would make a comment about her shortcomings and then find some humour in it, a delightful smile lighting her face, exposing a perfect set of white teeth, one of Ella's best features.

Debbie cut to the chase. "Ella, tell me what's wrong. You've gone through your whole life like this, and I've heard you laugh many times about your plight. What can I help you with?"

A tear welled up in Ella's eye and she wiped it away before it could slide down her cheek. "I don't know who else to turn to. You're my only real friend. If I don't pay the landlord soon, we're going to get evicted. And Garnet's in the hospital thinking everything's okay. I can't tell him it isn't, he'd get too upset, and he doesn't need this bad news before he goes in for major brain surgery." Now the tears were streaming down Ella's cheeks and she made no attempt to stop them. She put her face in her hands and began sobbing.

Debbie moved closer to Ella and put her arm around her. In spite of her tunnel-vision-like focus on business, she was moved by Ella's plight.

Debbie offered Ella a tissue. "Okay, okay, sweetie. We're going to get you out of this jam. And if you're worried about Garnet, he doesn't need to know. Let's get you home now. You tell me how much you need and I'll write you a cheque."

Debbie gave the signal to Don and he pulled the car forward. Ella and Debbie walked arm-in-arm to the waiting vehicle. Ella thanked Debbie ten times before they got in the car. As they drove Ella home, Debbie felt the hollow feeling in her heart begin to fill.

Chapter Nine

The year was 2003, and it was the middle of winter. A frigid minus 33 with the wind chill. Outside, the wind whistled and the snow drifted. Garnet sat on a couch with Ella and two of their friends in a small two-bedroom apartment. Ella stared at the TV. Susan slept in the bedroom. They had ended up there after they both lost their jobs and ran out of money. The landlord had evicted them and they were between apartments. Garnet sat in the kitchen, working on a music composition. He was composing a piano piece he was hoping to impress his music teacher with. For inspiration, he looked out at the blowing snow. Then he felt it. The aura came, a haze enveloping his senses. *Shit*, he thought. He knew with auras usually came seizures. His eyes glazed over and he stood up, walking like a robot around the kitchen. He felt like he was seeing himself from another pair of eyes in the room, like he was spiritually removed from himself. He wondered if he was dead and having flashbacks of his life.

Ella noticed the change instantly and walked into the kitchen, their two friends momentarily diverted from their show.

Like a zombie, Garnet walked to the front door, put on a pair of his friend's shoes, and prepared to embrace the storm. For protection from the elements, he wore a pair of sweatpants and a blue short-sleeved T-shirt, screen-printed with the Nike logo 'Just Do It.'

Ella recognized instantly that Garnet was having a psychomotor seizure and picked up her pace, stumbling and falling into Garnet as she reached the door. From his pair of eyes in the corner of the room, Garnet watched.

"No you don't, sweetie," Ella said, knowing full well her husband had no idea what he was doing or where he was.

She took his arm and led him to the couch.

Ella knew that psychomotor seizures, while impairing consciousness, also allowed people to function on auto-mode and often perform abnormal, violent, or criminal acts. She was thankful Garnet's acts thus far were only of the abnormal kind, as she sat with him on the couch and motioned for Rick to call 911. By the time the ambulance arrived, Garnet was making a whooping noise, his head bobbing from side to side, his body convulsing. A grand mal was announcing itself in fine fashion. Garnet shook violently on the couch, tongue dangling from his mouth. His eyeballs rolled back in his head so that only the whites of his eyes were visible.

Ella, in her attempts to contain him, was rewarded with a left cross to the cheekbone. She instinctively rubbed the wound, momentarily distracted from trying to contain Garnet. He sprang forward, pitching himself hard face-first on the carpet. He went stiff as a board.

Paramedics revived him en route to the hospital.

"I'm sooo, sooo sorry, honey," he said, waking up to see his wife and daughter at his bedside. He slowly cleared his head.

His wife leaned over and kissed him on the head. "Just another nightmare," she said.

Garnet was bewildered. He wondered why he was reliving in nightmares every violent seizure episode he had ever had in his life. Was someone trying to tell him something? Was the end near?

Susan sat down and kissed her dad on the cheek. She smiled at him. The smile wiped away any negative thoughts.

At least for the moment.

Garnet noticed his wife looked particularly perky that day. "What's up?" he asked.

Ella smiled, revealing those perfect teeth, but had promised herself she wouldn't say anything about the loan until Garnet was well out of the woods. "I'm just happy today, dear. We should always keep a positive attitude anyway," she said.

Susan switched on the TV. Cartoons. Reruns of *The Flintstones*. Garnet was surprised the TV worked, and was about to ask when Ella quieted him by putting her finger to her lips. She knew it was a gift from Debbie and Garnet did not need to know this right now. She didn't want him to begin questioning financial matters when he was about to undergo major brain surgery. Ella picked up a women's magazine that had been left behind by one of Garnet's former roommates. She had heard there were complications with the patient's lung transplant, but did not want to think beyond that.

Although, she noticed, it had been over a week and the woman had not returned.

She read the magazine while Susan and her dad watched *The Flintstones*. Garnet looked at his wife from the corner of his eye. He was reminded of how they first met.

As the two had become closer, Ella split from her boyfriend, and Garnet noticed her feelings toward him were beginning to change. One day, while walking home from church, Ella held his hand. Once he realized their relationship had changed, he spent three sleepless nights devising a plan to propose to her.

It was during dinner at a French restaurant that Garnet bent down on one knee and proposed. After she accepted, patrons of the restaurant applauded. He thought of the blush that had crept up Ella's cheeks, and smiled to himself.

His wife looked at him from the corner of her eye and winked.

She doesn't miss a beat, he thought.

A little while later Dr. Carsdale came in. Garnet flicked off the TV. Susan left the bedside and stood by the door. Ella put down the magazine and listened intently as Dr. Carsdale began discussing the analysis of the brain monitoring data. He concluded that Garnet would be undergoing brain surgery in a few weeks. Garnet could see his wife's brow furrow, and it seemed like his daughter was holding her breath.

Chapter Ten

It wasn't lost on Ella how many stares she received as she and Susan sat down and prepared for the day's sermon. The last of the congregation was now seated and the priest checked his microphone.

He opened a Bible, marked his place, and looked out at the congregation. Their chatter died down. The soft wail of a baby could be heard in the back row as he began to speak. The acoustics of the ornate building gave the cry a soft echo.

"Today we are going to talk about a passage from Luke 6:31," he said.

The baby's crying grew louder.

The audience members opened their bibles and found the passage.

From her seat in the third row, Susan counted the number of people sitting in the first row. She felt a sense of alienation as she looked at her mother's furrowed brow.

"Do onto others as you would have them do onto you," the priest said.

Ella looked across the aisle at one of her friends. The woman caught Ella's stare, pretended not to notice, and stared at the priest. As he talked about the importance of understanding that all people were created equal, Ella wondered how many good Christians were in attendance. She knew why people looked at her without acknowledging her or, worse still, ignored her completely. They thought she was less than they were, that she didn't have anything to offer. However, post-high school, Ella had had her intelligence tested and the result was that she possessed above-average intelligence. At that young age, she had her doubts about her intelligence, and she was relieved to learn she was not stupid.

She was also determined to live her life not through a mirror of other people's perceptions. She would define herself on her own terms, and let the arrogant people who judged her poorly go straight to hell, she thought, as the priest made a comment about the path to heaven.

She immediately tried to retract that thought as the priest's eyes moved around the audience, finally stopping at Ella.

She looked down at her hands in shame, intuitively feeling the discomfort of her daughter, and put her arm around her. Susan acknowledged the gesture with a smile.

Ella's mind started to drift as the priest went on, and she missed the entire second half of the sermon. Instead, she said a few prayers for her husband.

As she exited the church, she noticed the people who had ignored her when she entered were still ignoring her. The sermon hadn't sunk in, it seemed. Ella's thoughts returned to Garnet as she walked home.

Chapter Eleven

"I like it," Ron said, standing in the galley-style kitchen. He was a mechanic, and the first thing he did when Debbie walked in with them was go outside and view the three-car garage. Debbie stayed inside with Linda, his wife. Debbie knew who wore the pants in the family. Although the property was nicely updated, priced well and well-located, the floor plan was a little flawed, and the kitchen style was probably not what Linda was looking for.

It was the end of a six-property tour. They discussed its pros and cons. Debbie believed the first property they viewed, while requiring a few more updates, was more what the couple were looking for.

However, although Ron thought it had potential, Linda was not convinced. Debbie knew this property would not work. "Well, I don't like it," Linda said, the grimace returning to her face. Ron looked exasperated, and Debbie could tell there was more going on in their personal lives than just a minor disagreement on houses. She knew from years of experience these disagreements were a manifestation of much bigger issues. She wondered how long they would stay together.

"I don't like it at all," Linda said again as they all stood in the kitchen. "The kitchen sucks. You know that's not what I'm looking for."

Ron the renovator had an answer. "Don't worry, we can open it up." He walked around the kitchen now as he spoke.

"Look, this here is not a load-bearing wall. We can knock it down, put the kitchen over here, and it will be nice and open."

"Why the hell would you want to renovate an already renovated home?" Linda asked.

"I'm just trying to give you what you want. The garage is perfect for me. And I can make the kitchen perfect for you."

Debbie had inched toward the living room as the conversation began, thinking the couple should be having this discussion without her. "Maybe it's better I wait outside while you discuss it," she offered.

"No, I want you here," Linda demanded. "You tell me if it makes sense what he's saying. Do you think we should renovate an already renovated kitchen? Why the hell should we rip apart new renovations?"

Debbie thought before she answered. She understood the game. Linda made a good point, but she knew Linda's game. She wanted Debbie's acknowledgement so Ron's opinion would be undermined and appear stupid or, at the very least, not very well thought through.

Debbie knew how to navigate these troubled waters. And she also knew part of the game was Linda's control issues. Regardless of the house, Linda had to win. Debbie knew, regardless of what she said, the couple would not be writing an offer on this house. And Debbie had to be careful she didn't get dragged into the middle of a domestic dispute. But she also had to keep Ron happy. After all, it was his money that would be buying the house.

"If both of you like this property enough, we can buy it for the right price, and Ron can do the renovations inexpensively, then it would have some upside," she said cautiously. "But, if we go back to the first house on the tour, you remember it already has the floor plan and kitchen you're looking for, and the garage Ron is looking for. And the price point would give you very good sweat equity upside after your renovations."

She thought her answer was diplomatic enough. She remembered that, although Linda had expressed mild dissatisfaction at the first property, her eyes had lit up at the mention of an open floor plan with a breakfast nook and island. Although she was unhappy with its original condition, after renovations it could be transformed into her dream kitchen.

But Ron seemed to be stuck on the triple-car heated garage. The first property only contained an oversized double. "I could do the renovations for cheap in this house," he said. "And give you the kitchen of your dreams."

"I don't want the kitchen of my dreams in this house," Linda said. "Don't you get it?"

"Well, what about the other property?" Ron asked. "Even Debbie says it probably has better upside potential after renovations. And the floor plan is exactly what we're looking for. It only has a double, but I can live with that."

Debbie inched her way to the front door. She sensed they were both using her comments to support their positions, and soon she might find herself in an untenable position.

For Linda, it was about winning. "No, I don't like that other property either. This isn't like buying a pair of socks, you know."

Ron should have known when to let it go. "Yeah, it's a house. You can't wear a house. But this is the thirtieth property we've looked at, and you always seem to find some problem.

Don't you know it's not a perfect world? In real estate you have to make compromises."

Linda's expression turned downright medieval. Debbie knew as she opened the front door that the fireworks display was about to start. However, she had to admit, Ron had a good point. One part of her wanted to hear how Linda would counter that argument.

"Well, I'm not prepared to make any compromises right now," Linda said.

The voice of reason won for Debbie. She knew when to step out of the ring. She closed the door behind her and walked to her car. The voices inside, instead of becoming less audible, could now be heard halfway down the block.

After thirty or so minutes of squabbling, the two appeared outside the house, both looking agitated and not speaking to one another. Ron's face was flushed, and Linda had lines of anger contorting her delicate features. She looked ready to explode and begin round two. On the trip to the couple's car, Debbie sat in the back with Linda and had Ron sit up front with Don. Normally, Debbie would have tried some casual small talk to try and lighten the mood, but on this day she didn't give a fuck.

She wondered about that now as Don pulled up the winding driveway to her home, after they dropped Ron and Linda off. Previously, she would have been disappointed if she was not able to tap dance around her client's moods and win them over with her persuasiveness, but today it didn't seem to bother her. She smiled in spite of herself.

Chapter Twelve

Garnet lay in a stretcher in his room, waiting to be wheeled into surgery. He had been prepped earlier and his bald head glistened in the afternoon sunlight. The previous day's snowstorms had given way to sunnier conditions and the sky was clear blue. It was a balmy twelve degrees Celsius outside and not a cloud could be seen. His head was angled toward the window and he looked out at the bright blue sky, hoping it was a sign of good things to come.

After some discussion, the doctors and nurses had left Garnet with his family for a few minutes. Ella and Susan stood alongside the stretcher, watching Garnet look out the window.

"Beautiful day out there today, honey," Ella said, trying to keep the mood light.

"Mom said she's taking me to McDonalds after you leave," Susan announced. "I love their milkshakes."

"That's good, honey," he said. "Great day to be outside." Garnet could see concern etched in their features.

"We'll go when it's all over," Ella said, knowing Garnet occasionally had a hankering for a Big Mac.

The realization that this might be the last time she would see her husband alive hit Ella hard, not for the first time.

Susan bent over and kissed Garnet. "I love you, daddy," she said. Then she turned and walked to the door.

"I love you too, honey," Garnet said as the door closed. He knew his daughter was taking pains to keep a positive front and did not want to be seen breaking down in tears in front of her father.

Ella felt emotion welling up inside of her. She was powerless to fight it. The tears streamed down her face and she began to sob softly.

"Come here, sweetie," Garnet said, extending his arm and pulling his wife toward him. He plucked a tissue off the bed table and handed it to her as she kissed him. "Everything is going to work out just fine. I promise you."

Ella embraced him, still sobbing softly. "I love you so much," she said. "I don't know how I could go on without you."

"You won't have to. And I love you too."

It was time. Janice walked in and ever so gently plucked a sobbing Ella from her husband's stretcher. Garnet could see Janice supporting his crying wife as porters wheeled him down the hall to the operating room. His daughter smiled and waved to him as the stretcher passed. He could see her wiping her eyes again, this time with a tissue.

He was surrounded by masked faces. One of them put a plastic breathing apparatus over his mouth. He heard a hissing sound and knew the anaesthetic was being administered.

"I want you to count backwards from twenty," Dr. Carsdale said.

"Twenty, nineteen, eighteen, seven teeeen, six teeeeeeennnnnn." Garnet felt blackness overcome him.

He was in his backyard with his mother. It was September, but it was warm and sunny. The wind blew gently and leaves flipped through the air, settling on the grass around him. He stood in a pair of cross-country skis and his mother gave him instructions, helping him with his balance.

"You go like this," she said, making long, striding motions with her legs. "And then bring your skis together, like this when you want to slow down." She pointed her toes together. "There. You try it," she said.

Garnet started going through the motions and she stopped him.

"No, not quite, longer sweeping strides, like this." She walked across the lawn, sweeping her legs along in long strides.

Garnet watched. Tried again.

"That's better," she said. "And put your skis together like this to slow down."

Garnet tried the slowing technique. As he did, he felt a swirling sensation in his head and his vision blurred.

He watched himself lose his balance from a pair of eyes in the distance, saw his mother run to him and grab his arm. She looked into his eyes and saw they were blank—a petit mal seizure and possibly the pre-curser to a much larger one. She unbuckled the skis and led him over to a lawn chair.

Garnet began convulsing rapidly, his head swinging violently from side to side, his muscles beginning to stiffen, his eyes drawing back into their sockets.

The pair of eyes watched him convulse and violently pitch around the lawn.

Whose eyes? he thought. *My eyes?*

His mother screamed and ran into the house to call 911. Garnet rolled around on the lawn, crashing into lawn chairs and tipping them over in the process. He felt a sharp pain in his head, then heard a cutting sound. It was as though a part of his brain had been cut away. He could feel the pain very distinctly, yet strangely the watching eyes were removed from it.

By this time, he had rolled up against the fence and it blocked his movement somewhat. He thrashed into the fence with such force it bounced his body backward. Then his momentum continued and he crashed into the fence again.

He heard the cutting sound again. It felt like another piece of his brain had been removed. The eyes watched and his body felt the searing pain of the second cut. He felt a thunderous thumping in his head. Now he was only dimly aware of the convulsing body in front of the pair of eyes. The pair of eyes suddenly winced in pain, feeling the searing pain of the second cut.

Then Garnet's mind went completely black and he felt nothing but the steady drumbeat rhythm in his head. With every thumping sound, he felt his senses dull, his reasoning power abandoning him, his mental faculties and motor functions diminishing. In the blackness, he could no longer see or feel his thrashing body. All the eyes saw was a pinhole-sized white light that seemed to come from far away. It grew dimmer and dimmer, and once again Garnet's mind was enveloped by blackness.

Dr. Carsdale looked down and admired his work. He had cut a clean opening in the left side of Garnet's head, which had given him access to the brain. He had removed what he believed was all the scar tissue. That meant the removal of the hippocampus, amygdale, and part of the temporal lobe. The eight-hour surgery had gone well, and Garnet's vitals, although sporadic in the beginning, had been normal throughout the remainder of the surgery. He looked down at his patient as one of the nurses suctioned some remaining blood from inside the head and checked his vitals again. They were normal.

"Stitch him up," he said to Bill knowing that Bill's expert suturing would leave only a small trace of a scar when everything had healed.

"Yes sir," Bill said. Carsdale left the operating room, believing the operation would prove to be a resounding success.

Chapter Thirteen

Garnet's eyes slowly opened. Through blurred vision, he could make out two female faces looking down at him. He had no idea who they were. He had no peripheral vision, only a little circle of light in front of his eyes. Tunnel vision. He was disoriented, and he felt the drumbeat in his head, a throbbing that produced blackness and excruciating pain. He thought he was going to pass out again.

"Sweetie, how are you feeling?" Ella said, a look of grave concern on her face.

Susan began to cry. She could tell something was not right with her dad.

Ella knew as well. The expression she saw in her husband's eyes was certainly not one of familiar recognition. He not only looked far gone, but also in a lot of pain. Her voice rose with concern.

"Garnet, Garnet, say something," she said.

Garnet did not recognise the voice, nor could he make sense of the words. The drumbeat intensified. He tried to talk. "Abbbrrt ya si gige abbbbrrrt ?" he asked the two faces peering down at him.

He thought he asked them where he was and what had happened to him, but, judging by their responses, he guessed it had probably not come out that way.

He tried again: "Wbbeeeert eeeeee yeee gigee ameee?"

The drumbeat in his head grew louder and more painful, drowning out what he thought were screams coming from the faces.

It seemed to him the right side of his face was completely caved in. He tried to raise his right hand. Nothing. He tried to move his right leg. Nothing. In his haze, he became convinced the entire right side of his body was no longer with him. He tried to move his head to see but could not.

The beat went on. He closed his eyes as the pain intensified, then opened them. The little white circle of vision had grown smaller. The screams grew faint.

Ella raced down the hall toward the nursing station, arriving at the same time as a porter wheeling a cart full of medication. They collided. Ella tripped over her feet just before reaching the cart and fell face first into it. The cart tipped over, sending pills flying everywhere. The porter stepped aside fast enough to avoid getting hit, but not fast enough to avoid backing into a food services employee with a tray of juices. The porter smashed into the juice cart and sent it rolling back toward the food services employee, who was not expecting it to come at him with such force. It hit him hard, sending the juices and the cart flying in the air. He fell backward on his ass, the cart and a lot of orange sticky liquid covering his blue uniform. He did not look happy.

Janice ran to Ella's aid. She was crumpled up on top of the medicine cart. Blood dripped from a small cut on her cheek, the point of impact.

The porter went to the aid of the food services employee. Other than an orange juice shower, he looked none the worse for wear. The porter helped the food services man to his feet.

He was not smiling, although the faint trace of a smile was detectable on the porter's mouth.

"Are you okay?" Janice asked Ella, helping her to her feet. "Here, let me get something for that cut."

"Uhhhh ... uhhhh ... Garnet," Ella said. The panic in Ella's voice was audible, and everyone stopped what they were doing. "Something is seriously wrong with Garnet," she said to Janice. "He's not making any sense at all. Please, please get help!"

Janice responded immediately, and within minutes a team of doctors were running down the hall towards Garnet's room.

"Are you okay, Mom?" Susan asked. She stood beside her mother and held the cotton baton to the small cut.

"It's Garnet I'm worried about, honey. I'm fine."

Carsdale and his team raced past them on their way to the operating room.

Something was definitely wrong.

In the operating room, Carsdale immediately ordered an MRI to determine what was happening inside Garnet's head. He saw it immediately. A throbbing artery. Clogged. About to burst. The upside was that Garnet was in the best place possible to suffer an ischemic stroke. The downside was that if doctors were not able to unclog the throbbing artery in short order, it could explode, causing irreparable damage, confining Garnet to a wheelchair for the rest of his life with limited brain function and motor skills; or worse still, kill him.

Carsdale knew he had a short window before the damage would be extensive and irreversible. He would need to administer a medication called tissue plasminogen activator, used in clot busting.

"Bring in an IV of TPA," he said. "Stat!"

He watched the brain activity on another MRI after the drug was administered intravenously. He breathed a sigh of relief when he saw the artery was no longer throbbing. It looked as if the TPA had worked. Now, the big question was, how long had the clogged artery cut off important blood supply to Garnet's brain, and what was the extent of the damage? After three hours of blood loss to the brain, damage is usually extensive and irreversible. He thought the stroke must have occurred at the end of Garnet's surgery. He certainly did not see anything abnormal during surgery, so his best guess was Garnet's stroke had lasted an hour or slightly longer.

But he couldn't be sure.

Chapter Fourteen

Garnet's vitals were checked, found to be normal, and he was wheeled into the intensive care unit.

Garnet opened his eyes slowly and noticed a flutter of activity around him. Janice was checking his IV and adjusting controls on the panel of monitors that surrounded him.

"Here, take this," she said, offering him some medication. Garnet watched her fuzzy image come into focus and a flicker of recognition crossed his mind.

He tried to speak but the words came out in an incomprehensible babble.

But he understood what she was saying. He reached for the pills with his right hand. It would not move. The right side of his face still felt like it was caved in, and he could not feel the entire right side of his body. He suspected he could not walk, and he knew he couldn't talk.

At least the drumbeat in his head had subsided. It had been replaced by a dull, aching pain.

He still had the tunnel vision, but his range of vision was much better.

He thought he knew who this person was. Janice Priestly, his nurse. Janice opened his mouth, deposited the anti-seizure medication, gently tilted his head back, and washed it down with water.

"Swallow," she said. "That's it."

Susan and Ella arrived the next day. "Honey, how do you feel?" Ella asked.

Garnet looked up at the blurry image in front of him and didn't know who she was.

"Honey, it's me, your wife. Do you recognize me? Sweetie, nod your head yes if you know who I am."

The face was still too blurry for Garnet to recognize. But he knew the voice. *My wife.* He tried to move his head. Nothing happened.

Ella could see him wincing. "Honey, try something else. Raise your right hand if you know it's me."

Garnet tried to move his right hand. It would not budge. He raised his left hand slowly and waved to his wife.

Ella couldn't stop the tears. Janice passed her a tissue. Ella sat down, held her husband's left hand, and gently kissed him on the cheek, sobbing.

Susan had also begun to cry, but she covered her face with a tissue so her father would not see. She slid over on the bed beside her mother, put her hand on her father's left arm, and kissed him on the cheek.

Garnet's vision improved enough to recognize his daughter. He tried to speak. Again, nothing. Susan could see the flicker of recognition on her father's contorted features and she smiled.

Dr. Carsdale walked in and opened his chart.

"Garnet, do you know who I am? Hold up your left index finger if you do."

Garnet held up his finger.

"Unfortunately I have some bad news. It appears that shortly after surgery you suffered a stroke. Now, the upside is that you were in the best place possible to suffer a stroke. Also the stroke was ischemic—a clogged artery—and not hemorrhagic, a ruptured artery."

Garnet's features darkened at this news. He had walked into the hospital on his own two feet, and now, not only could he barely think, the entire right side of his face and body were paralyzed. He couldn't walk or talk. It seemed to him his life had gone from bad to worse.

A black cloud of depression settled over him.

"In any event, we were able to unclog the artery, but we aren't sure how long the stroke lasted and how much damage it's done. In other words, we don't know at this time what kind of recovery you'll be able to make, if any."

Ella picked up two more tissues and blew her nose, wiping away a few tears.

"About seventy-five percent of stroke survivors are disabled to the point where it decreases their employability. We will monitor your progress for a week or so, and then you'll be moved to the stroke unit, where we will assign a speech and physical therapist to you, and maybe a psychologist to help with your recovery as well. Do you understand all this?"

Garnet looked at Carsdale. There was a long moment of silence before Garnet's eyes showed understanding and Carsdale left.

Chapter Fifteen

Ella sat in a downtown office boardroom and looked down at the sheets of paper in front of her, confusion etched in her brow. She re-read one of the questions. She had read it once a few seconds earlier, but her mind had forgotten it. She read the multiple-choice options in front of her, and then her mind drifted again. She noticed how the twenty or so people seated around the boardroom table intently studied their exams, scribbling answers.

Ella daydreamed about her past, growing up in Edmonton with her alcoholic parents.

Although big drinkers, her parents ran a pretty tight household. Her father, an aircraft mechanic, paid more attention to her three other siblings than to Ella. He considered her mentally challenged. And, other than a few comments about what he perceived to be her limitations, she could not remember any overt cruelty at his hands.

Her mother, a social butterfly, was always entertaining friends. Her mother was embarrassed about her challenged daughter and as a result, Ella was excluded from a lot of entertaining.

Ella's mother died at forty six due to breast cancer that spread to the ovaries, eventually poisoning her entire body. Ella was twelve years old at the time.

Her father remarried a few years later.

Her stepmother, who had merged three kids from a previous union into the household, openly despised Ella.

She put ideas into Ella's father's head that Ella was a liar and a manipulator. For whatever reason, her father seemed to buy it, and all but abandoned Ella during her critical child-rearing years.

Her father died of a brain tumour when Ella was thirty-five. He was survived by Ella's stepmother, with whom communication had long ago ceased.

Other than some lingering bad memories of her stepmother, what had stuck with Ella over the years was the misdiagnosis of her condition. Doctors had diagnosed her as being mentally retarded. She knew that she had short-term memory issues and attention deficit disorder, but surely this was pretty far from being mentally retarded.

But, like anything, if you listen to something long enough, you start to believe it. So, through the first sixteen years of her life, she had believed herself mentally retarded. And, although post-high school aptitude testing had indicated an above average intelligence, she still had a hard time discarding the notion of being mentally retarded from her mind.

She tried to push it out of her mind now as she read the multiple-choice question for a third time. She checked an answer she wasn't sure of and then moved on to the next question. She tried to concentrate, but her thoughts turned to the preliminary exam, and the fact that it had taken her seven attempts to pass that one, and only with tutoring did she succeed.

Doubts crept into her mind as she remembered failing the final the first time. She wondered, at $100 per exam, how many tries she would need to pass it.

Her right knee and leg ached with arthritic pain. She shook the leg as she checked an answer that she did not feel confident about.

Focus, she said to herself, and studied the next question. She was worried about her husband and unsure about his chances for recovery after the stroke. She knew if he did not recover, she was their only chance at paying the bills.

She had to pass this exam, had to succeed at this. She had to push past this negative thinking and concentrate.

She was about twelve questions from the finish line when she heard the instructor announce, "One minute left."

In panic mode, Ella feverishly checked off all the remaining multiple-choice questions, guessing at every one of them. She was the last person to leave the exam room.

As she stood outside waiting for her bus, she felt sure she had failed.

Again.

As the bus pulled up to the stop, she wondered what she was going to do next.

Chapter Sixteen

"So you're one of the top hitters at ReMax," Paul said, admiring Debbie as he sipped his martini. He crunched an olive, adjusted his position in the high-back leather chair, and continued. "I admire people like you, who can accomplish their goals. You fit right into my vision of the capitalist machine."

Debbie smiled. Capitalist machine? *Great, now people are comparing me to a machine.* She thought of a caged rat, running on one of those steel exercise wheels. He would run, run and run until he completely exhausted himself. Then he would crawl off the wheel, take a drink of water, and eye the wheel suspiciously, wondering if he should hop back on. After a while, he would hop back on the wheel. Going nowhere, tiring himself out, yet not knowing why he was running.

That was Debbie's image of the capitalist machine.

At the very least, it was a view of her unbridled pursuit of material gain. Debbie wondered why she hadn't drawn that conclusion earlier.

Before Debbie could respond, Paul spoke again. He seemed content, at least for now, to listen to himself speak and admire her sexiness. "You know what you want and you get it. How many deals, on average, do you do in a month?"

This threw Debbie momentarily. She picked up her glass of white wine, took a sip, and eyed him suspiciously before answering. *Where do I find these guys?* But she knew where she had found him. On Plenty of Fish, the Internet dating site. *It should be called Plenty of Freaks*, she thought as she wondered how to respond. It seemed to her Paul was not only impressed by her money, but maybe that was all he was interested in.

In his profile, he had described himself as an independent, self-made businessman who loved to travel, was a hopeless romantic and a deep thinker. It turned out he lived in the basement of his mother's house and was trying to launch a website selling sex toys and porn videos. Much of his time was spent playing Xbox video games. Debbie wondered who had written his profile.

"Oh, I don't count the number of deals I do. That's bad luck."

"You must have some idea. Like would it be ten or more, or less than ten?"

Debbie was getting impatient. In her quest to find love, she had turned to Internet dating sites. And now she wondered why. The last six guys she had met through Plenty of Freaks were not at all what she was looking for.

She wanted a guy who would like her for who she was and not how much money she made. She wriggled in her chair and turned her attention to her phone. She set the call mode from vibrate to ring, and waited for Lisa's call. It must be an hour by now.

Prior to the date, as per her usual protocol, she had instructed Lisa to call her after an hour. If she was enjoying herself, she would ignore the call. If she wasn't having fun, she would answer the call as if it were a client, make her apologies, and leave. She couldn't remember exactly how long they had been talking, but she knew it must be very close to an hour. She looked at the phone, willing it to ring.

"In this business, people don't care what you know until they know that you care. So, if I'm concerned with dollars, my clients will see that and I won't be successful. I have to demonstrate to them that I care, that I want the best for them, and I'm not concerned with commissions."

"That sounds like a load of bullshit," Paul said, now appearing agitated he wasn't getting the answers he wanted. He waved the young and attractive waitress over, ordered two more drinks, and carried on. "Everyone cares about money. Anyone who says different is a liar. Now, I'm not saying you're a liar, I'm just saying you're not telling the whole truth."

Debbie wondered if in her case, he was right. And that bothered her for the first time. Previously, she did not think she would have cared if someone insinuated she was a capitalist pig.

In fact, in some ways, she was proud of it. It insulated her from feelings, feelings that always turned painful and led to suffering.

In any event, she was tired of listening to this dipstick.

The phone rang. It was Lisa. *Thank God*, Debbie thought, and answered. "Hi, Elaine, how are you?" A brief pause. "Listen, hang on one sec, okay? I'll be right with you." Debbie put her hand over the phone receiver. "Listen, Paul, it was a real pleasure to meet you." She slapped $30 on the table, more than enough to cover her two glasses of wine. "I have to leave. One of my clients wants to write an offer."

"So fast," Paul said. "I thought you didn't care about money."

He was saying something else as Debbie left the bar, but she couldn't make out what it was. She knew one thing. She didn't like the tone of it; and by the way he had begun slurring his speech, it seemed as if the four martinis had taken their toll.

As Don drove her home, Debbie wondered what she was going to do with her life.

Chapter Seventeen

Garnet sat at his piano as the instructor looked on. He was being examined for concert level piano. He would have to play five pieces of music, including Bach pieces from memory, and do them flawlessly in order to successfully accomplish one of his lifelong goals. Ever since he could remember, Garnet had wanted to be a concert level pianist.

The left side of his head felt cold. The right side of his body and his face felt stiff. He looked at the keyboard, then back at the instructor.

"Are you all set?" the instructor asked.

All Garnet could see of the instructor was a small head in the corner of the room. He thought he could make out a smile as well. Everything around the instructor was blackness. Garnet reached inside his memory, trying to find the notes he had memorized.

Images of musical notes swept through his mind, but they were jumbled. *Concentrate. Pull it together.* He strained to try and remember the first piece. Nothing would come, and a throbbing pain took hold of his brain. He felt hot. Beads of perspiration dripped down his head. Then he felt cold. He shivered and tried to clear his head.

"Are you ready? You can begin anytime."

He looked at the keyboard again and started playing. He listened as he played and noticed the instructor's brow begin to furrow. *This isn't right.* It sounded like the music he played was a blend of at least three of the five pieces.

He could tell from the instructor's expression he was way off the mark.

The instructor stopped him. "Garnet, why don't you compose yourself and try again?"

Garnet opened his mouth to speak. No words came out. *What's happening to me?* He re-focused on the piano. This time his mind went completely black and the keyboard faded into oblivion. He tried to move his right hand to open his eyes, but it was hard as a rock. The left side of his face felt the same. He tried the left hand. It worked. He brought it to his face, rubbing his eyes, as if that would bring his vision back. He moved his hand away and looked to where he thought the instructor was sitting. Total blackness.

He felt panic and nausea well up inside of him. He could not remember a single piece of music. His life's work was erased from his mind. He searched his memory again for the notes.

Nothing.

What about advanced rudiments of music? he thought. He remembered not being able to do that exam because of pain in his arms. He tried to contain the panic and nausea now surging through his body. Rudiments, he said to himself. He reached into the depths of his mind. Again nothing. Complete and total blank. Then suddenly something did flash into his mind, but not the notes he was looking for. It was a complete musical production of a death and rebirth of sorts. The acts, the titles, the music flooded in like a swiftly moving tide and he struggled to retain them.

But the information overwhelmed him.

"Are you okay?" he heard the instructor ask.

Garnet was not okay. He felt like he was going to be sick. Panic and nausea suddenly overtook him and he opened his mouth to scream. No sound came out. But he could feel it coming. Vomit.

"Are you okay, Garnet?" he heard again.

It was Dr. Carsdale. The doctor looked down at Garnet, whose face was now turning a pale green color. "Wake up, you're having a bad dream."

Garnet opened his eyes, barely recognizing the man standing over him. He started coughing and vomited, spewing a yellowish liquid, which splashed off Dr. Carsdale's chest, soaking Garnet and his bed on the rebound.

Carsdale jumped back as the projectile vomit spewed forth, but not quite in time to avoid it. He grimaced but immediately motioned to the ICU nurses, who came running over to offer their assistance. With gloved hands, Janice held Garnet's head forward, making sure the yellow liquid found a home inside a bucket she had brought over.

With the situation under control, Dr. Carsdale left in pursuit of some clean clothes.

Fifteen minutes later, housekeeping staff cleaned up the mess and Garnet was moved momentarily while the bedsheets were changed. They also replaced the two ice packs on the sutured side of his head to keep his temperature down. New pillows were placed around him, propping him up so his limbs would not dangle off the bed. Various monitors were plugged back in.

He realized he had had a nightmare, but also realized to his horror that the nightmare was true. He could not remember a single piece of music he had memorized, particularly the ones he had studied so hard to achieve his concert level pianist status.

He tried to remember what he once knew about advanced rudiments of music, and drew another blank.

His heart sank.

He couldn't walk, talk or remember anything. His vision was limited and his mind was murky, much worse than it had been when he was admitted. The now-familiar black cloud of depression settled over him again, and he seriously started to wonder if there was really any point at all in living.

After a short nap, porters took Garnet in a wheelchair to the stroke rehabilitation wing. Carsdale wanted to get him up and around quickly to encourage circulation in his muscles. While he was in bed, pumps had been attached to his legs, which would compress and decompress to promote circulation.

As he was being wheeled around, he started to feel a little better. He passed a man in a wheelchair who had lost both his legs above the knees, and the short encounter gave him inspiration. As he passed, the old man smiled and said, "Have an awesome day, young man."

Garnet was wheeled into a large room containing an assortment of occupational therapy equipment. The porter pushed him to a set of bars that resembled parallel bars, but were much lower.

"Adam will be in momentarily," he said, and left.

Garnet stared at the bars in front of him and wondered how in the world he would ever get his legs moving. He still could not feel his entire right side, including the right side of his face, which felt hideously contorted.

"Okay, let's get you up here," Adam said as he approached Garnet. He was with a young woman of about twenty-two, whom he introduced as Myrna, his student assistant.

The two gently lifted Garnet to the bars. His muscles felt hard as rock as they positioned him. Myrna held his right shoulder and Adam was on the left side. Myrna smiled, showing her brilliant white teeth and a twinkle in her blue eyes. "You can do it, Garnet," she said, encouraging him to move his legs.

Garnet willed his legs to move and nothing happened. He strained again and felt the left leg obey while the right leg began to drag along the floor. His right arm felt stiff, but seemed to inch forward with his will. He felt a tingling sensation in the right side of his body. Both arms slipped and he was about to crash land. That's when he noticed for the first time that Adam and Myrna were no longer supporting him. They were there in a heartbeat, steadying his arms before they could slip through the bars.

"Don't worry," Adam said. "We're right here. You're doing well. Keep going."

Garnet felt beads of sweat begin to form on his forehead as he took a deep breath and began again. He grunted as he inched his way along the bars. He noticed that his right leg no longer dragged. It was actually taking steps in unison with the left leg. Garnet was also aware that his right arm was developing some feeling. From the numbness and near-zero feeling on the right side of his body, he now felt the tingling again. A smile contorted his features and his demeanour changed. *I'm doing it. I'm walking on my own.* He could see Adam and Myrna, now at the end of the bars, smiling and encouraging him. He grunted and shifted his way along the bars. The tingling feeling now encompassed his facial muscles and his smile felt less contorted. He wanted to say something. "I doooan it," he managed.

He listened to the words as he spoke them. *That was close*, he thought. *Maybe I'll try again*. He also noticed, quite suddenly, his field of vision had improved dramatically. He now only had small black shadows on the outside perimeters of his vision, and it seemed they were beginning to turn grey. Garnet smiled again as he strained.

He was now two thirds of the way along the bars, and his motion had become much less laboured. While he still needed his arms to provide some support for his legs, it seemed the legs now had a will of their own, and they wanted to walk.

"I'm doin' it," Garnet said emphatically.

Adam and Myrna, at the other end of the bars, looked incredulous. Never before had they witnessed this kind of a rapid recovery from stroke. Usually the process took months or years, and in many cases patients were never able to completely regain total control of their motor functions.

"Look, I'm doin' it," Garnet said again, the decibel level of his voice increasing with his excitement.

"Yes, you are," Adam responded. "Keep going."

They understood me, Garnet thought as he continued. "I can walk ... and talk again," he said out loud.

"Yes, you can," Myrna said, motioning him to continue forward.

Garnet could see the end of the bars now, a few feet away. Tears of joy streamed down his cheeks as he continued. On the last stretch, he took a deep breath and released his arms from the bars. His legs quivered, but held. He was now standing on his own two feet. He slowly took a step with his right foot. It held. He tried the left. It held. He saw the outstretched arms in front of him. The smiling faces.

He thought he saw a tear forming in Myrna's right eye. He had two, maybe three steps ahead of him. He thought he had the strength to quicken the pace, and attempted to walk faster. That's when his right foot tripped up the left and he careened forward.

Myrna and Adam grabbed him before he could slam face-first into the padded mat below. "Way to go, way to go," Adam said. "I can't believe you just did that."

Chapter Eighteen

Ella had received a phone call earlier in the day from Dr. Carsdale. He said Garnet had performed admirably during rehabilitative therapy. In fact, Carsdale, while cautioning that Garnet still had a long road ahead of him, described the events to her as nothing short of a miracle.

The news had lifted her spirits immensely; particularly since the first call she received was from the instructor at World Financial Group, who had rather tactlessly informed her she had failed her second attempt at the exam. He also pointed out her mark was lower than her first attempt. This news had spiralled Ella into a mental funk, until Carsdale called, lifting her spirits.

She stood in an elevator of the Holiday Inn Hotel, on her way up to the seventh floor, where she was about to be interviewed for a chambermaid position. The elevator doors opened, and she stepped out into the hallway. *Was it room 713?* A heavy-set man accompanied by a woman walked toward her in the hallway. The man's eyes were rolling in his head, saliva dripped from his mouth, and he grinned from ear to ear. He walked pigeon-toed and with a slight limp. *He looks retarded*, Ella thought as they neared.

The man looked at Ella with recognition, as if he was identifying something in common they shared.

"Hyah, hyah," he said, smiling as they passed.

Ella smiled at the man, but did not say anything. She wondered if she knew him as she knocked on the door to room

713. A wet man clad only in a white towel answered the door after about six knocks. "Can I help you?" he asked, annoyed.

"I ... I ... I'm here for the interview," Ella said, embarrassed.

"What interview?"

Ella looked at the door number and it registered. "Sorry, I think I have the wrong room."

"You definitely have the wrong room," the man said, slamming the door in her face.

Ella felt the hot redness of embarrassment color her cheeks as she moved down to hall to 715.

Inside, she sat down and faced a man with a well-trimmed beard, black suit, and red tie. He peered at her through horn-rimmed glasses, shuffled some papers, found Ella's application, and studied it.

Ella squirmed in her seat and felt her cheeks flush red.

"It says here you finished a culinary class at SAIT." He paused and Ella squirmed some more. "How come it took you three years to complete a two-year course?"

Ella thought honesty was the best policy. "Um, my hand-eye coordination is not that great, and I have problems with short-term memory," she said. "But I did get through it and got a certificate."

The man looked at the application again before responding. He was not, after all, interviewing for a CEO position. "Okay. This is a cleaning position, not a cooking job. How are your cleaning skills?" he asked.

Ella thought of the disarray of her household. "Very good, when I focus on it."

"When you focus on it?" he asked. "Do you have trouble focusing on things?"

Ella thought about her father and stepmother interrogating her as a child and how her mind would draw a complete blank. They would ask her to remember certain things. She wanted to remember the things they asked, to end the interrogation, but her mind would not allow it. The pressure of the interrogation created a blank space in her mind.

"When I was young, I was diagnosed with attention deficit disorder," she said candidly. "Also, I was hyper, and my mom used to say I would climb kitchen cabinets in the middle of the night. I think they should have named me Tas."

The man laughed in spite of himself, impressed by her honesty.

"But I'm much better now," Ella said. "I find my focus is better and I can sit for long periods and sketch pictures, where before I would have never been able to do that."

He looked over the application again. "Tas, as in the Tasmanian devil?" he asked.

"Yes," Ella said, and smiled.

"What do you figure is your best quality, and why do you think you are right for this position?"

Most of the redness had left her cheeks, and she felt more relaxed. "My best quality is my honesty. I'm right for this position because my husband's in hospital recovering from a stroke and we desperately need the money. I don't know if he will be employable when he leaves."

There was a long pause. Ella was sure the last questions were trick questions and she had blown the interview.

"When can you start?"

Two hours later, Ella was up on the 16th floor of the high-rise hotel. Two Mexican chambermaids had smirked and whispered something to each other as she walked passed them with her cleaning cart. A Filipino woman, Zigga, accompanied her as they entered a vacated room.

The woman talked incessantly.

"You must go fast," she said. "Very fast. Boss man wants us go fast. The last room too slow. You pick up, go fast on this one. Go start bathroom, get garbage and towels. I be in here." The woman motioned Ella into the bathroom and began stripping the sheets from the two beds in the room.

Cleaning the first room, Ella had become confused when Zigga began barking orders at her. She had accidentally carried dirty towels back into the bathroom and replaced the clean ones. Zigga was scornful at this, which only confused Ella even more. On the way out, she left a stack of clean towels on a bureau and a large ring of keys. She was just about to lock the door behind her when Zigga had said, "What you do? Don't close door. You don't have keys. Here give 'em to me," and she snatched away the key ring as Ella reached for it.

In the bathroom, Ella looked distractedly out the window. She listened to the buzz of traffic, watched the cars, and followed the tiny people as they went about their business in the streets below.

She heard voices and realized someone else had entered the room. She walked out of the bathroom to see what was going on.

A young man and woman stood with their luggage by the door, looking as confused as Ella.

"You in wrong room," Zigga said to them. "This one being cleaned."

The man looked at his key and motioned to the room number. "No, I think I'm in the right room," he said, producing his key and presenting it to Zigga so she could see the numbers matched. "Listen, we're exhausted. Can you tell me when you'll have it ready?"

"Fi minutes," Zigga said.

After they left, Zigga started barking orders to Ella again. "You quick in bathroom. People need room."

Ella stared at her blankly.

"You quick in bath. They want room fast," she said. "Go now."

Ella went into the bathroom. She looked at the clump of dirty towels in the bath and bent down to pick them up. As she walked to the cleaning cart, two of them slipped from her grip. She didn't notice.

"You get towels," Zigga instructed her, now clearly annoyed. She picked the dirty towels off the floor and handed them to Ella, who by this time had turned around and begun reaching for clean towels. She still hadn't noticed the dirty towels and had misunderstood Zigga.

"What you do? Take these," Zigga said, stuffing the dirty towels in Ella's hands as she swung around with clean towels. The dirty towels took her by surprise and she opened her arms to take them, dropping her stack of clean towels on the floor in the process. As she bent to pick them up, she bumped into the cart, sending it bouncing off the hallway wall.

Two bottles of liquid cleaner fell off the cart, slowly spilling their contents on the burgundy carpet.

Zigga had had enough. "What you fuckin' do?" she asked, her voice growing louder. "How you clean fast? All you make is mess."

Ella walked toward the draining bottles of cleaner, but Zigga was already there, picking them up. Most of the contents had emptied onto the carpet, leaving a greenish-white, foamy stain.

Ella looked at the stain and froze. She could hear Zigga yelling but couldn't understand. She stared at the diminutive woman, who was jumping and flailing her arms. Ella didn't know what to do. Her mind went completely blank and she smiled at Zigga.

"What you problem?" Zigga asked, bending down to scrub the carpet stain.

Ella only stared at her with a widening smile. She had no idea what to do next.

Zigga's words had smoothly blended into a continuous stream of incomprehensible gibberish as she continued to rant. But the next two words she heard came from a male voice, and she understood them perfectly well.

"You're fired," the small Asian man now standing beside her said. "Get out of here! Now!"

As Ella walked to her bus stop, she wondered what she was going to do next. But then her thoughts turned to Garnet and his miraculous progress, and she smiled again.

"It's only money," she said to no one in particular.

Chapter Nineteen

Garnet stared at the image in front of him and tried to recollect the name of the animal.

"Elephant," he said after pausing momentarily.

"Good," said Eve, his therapist. She pulled out another card. Garnet looked at it.

"Dog," he said.

"Right," she said, turning the card over and pulling out another one. The next card was intended to divert the learner's attention away from the current theme. It was the image of a cheque for $5000 with Garnet's name on it. Garnet looked at the image with a puzzled expression. He scratched the left side of his head with his good hand.

"Take your time, Garnet," she said. "It will come to you."

But it wasn't coming to him. His brow furrowed, the creases in his head becoming deeper. He felt a bead of perspiration form on his forehead as he racked his brain. He wiped at it with his good hand and searched Eve's eyes, as if it was there he could find the answer.

Finally he said, "Can, can you give me a hint?"

"Okay," Eve said. "It starts with a C."

Garnet pondered it some more. He vaguely remembered seeing something like this in the past, but could not remember what it was for.

"Can you give me the second letter?" he asked.

"H," Eve said.

Suddenly it came to him. "Cheque," he said.

"Very good, Garnet. I knew you would get it. Now, do you remember what this cheque is used for?"

The more Garnet thought about it, the more he realized he didn't have a clue. "No idea," he said after a long silence.

"The banks issue them and we use them to buy things and pay bills. They're like money," Eve explained.

"What do we need money for if these things are like money?" Garnet asked.

"When we buy things using cheques, the money value of the cheques is withdrawn from our bank accounts," Eve said.

"Oh, I see," Garnet said. "So we obviously still need money in our account to cover the cheque?"

"Now you're getting it," Eve said.

Garnet's brain was starting to feel tired from this session and his legs ached from his recent physiotherapy. But he knew all this was part of the recovery, and he would have to endure. He was coming to the end of an hour of identifying cards, and he was starting to get anxious for the session to end. He could still feel a light throbbing in his head, and it bothered him that he did not know what a cheque was used for. He wondered what else he had forgotten.

He yawned and tried to stand, but the stiffness in his legs prevented him from moving too far and he plopped back in his wheelchair before Eve could respond.

"Whoa there soldier," she said, and steadied his shoulder with her hand. "Why don't we wrap up this session. We'll carry on tomorrow."

She put away the cards and a porter came in to take Garnet to the psychological counseling unit, a critical component of his recovery.

Garnet was wheeled into an office where a man introduced himself as Dr. Fritz. Garnet guessed he liked to be called that, as he didn't mention his first name; although Garnet could see by the placard on his desk it was Wolfgang. Garnet wondered if Dr. Fritz liked his first name.

Behind his desk, Garnet could see a wall of framed accomplishments, a Ph.D degree, and various other certificates. He found the wall intimidating. Dr. Fritz began the session.

"How are you feeling today, Garnet?" he asked, turning on a tape recorder as he spoke.

"I'm okay," Garnet said. "A little stiffness in the legs and my head hurts a little."

"How did your session with Eve go today?"

"Um, okay, I suppose. I couldn't remember what a cheque is used for and that kind of bothered me. But I'm thrilled with my walking progress. I thought I might be stuck in this wheelchair forever." Garnet looked at his toes as he spoke and noticed for the first time his left shoe was untied.

"Yes, your progress was much quicker than expected, on all levels," Dr. Fritz said. "We weren't expecting your motor skills or your brain function to return so quickly, and I think it's nothing short of a miracle that you're doing as well as you are. How did it make you feel when you couldn't remember what a cheque is used for?"

"Not that good," Garnet said, bending down to try and tie his shoe. When he finally got his aching arms to the laces, he realized he didn't have a clue how to tie them. He tried to dig in his brain for the answer. Nothing came. He fumbled with the laces.

"Are you okay?" Dr. Fritz asked. "You need some help?"

"Ahhh ... I can't remember how to tie my shoes," Garnet finally said with a helpless expression.

"Let me see," Dr. Fritz said, taking the laces in his hands. He went through the motions, pausing before every loop to show Garnet exactly what he was doing. "There," he said, tying the lace. "Do you want to try it?"

Garnet wasn't sure he had the sequence imprinted in his brain, and asked Dr. Fritz to do it again. Finishing a second time, Dr. Fritz looked up at Garnet. "Do you want me to do it again, or would you like to try it now?"

"Can I wait?" Garnet asked, not feeling all that confident. "Can I practice and do it next time for you?"

"No problem at all," Dr. Fritz said, resuming his seated position. "You show me when you're good and ready. Now then, let's continue. I want to try and get a picture of your mental state. Can you tell me exactly how you're feeling? Do you feel a sense of hopelessness at all?"

He did feel hopeless when it came to tying his shoe. He also felt hopeless when he did not know what a cheque was for. And, initially there was an overwhelming sense of depression. But he had noticed this initial depression fading, particularly when he thought of his family and his walking progress. Garnet guessed Dr. Fritz was trying to determine if he was clinically depressed, a symptom he was told many stroke victims suffered.

"No, not really," he said. "At least, it's not overwhelming. I do hope to make a full recovery and pursue a Bachelor of Fine Arts degree in Music. I also have a musical production in my head that I'm going to finish composing and have performed."

Dr. Fritz paused and pondered before continuing. He wondered if Garnet was suffering from Anosognosia, the inability to acknowledge his physical and mental impairments.

"Do you recognize that you have some impairments as a result of your stroke?" he asked.

"Well, yeah, that's obvious," Garnet said. "But that's not to say I don't plan on making a complete recovery and pursuing my passion."

"What is your recollection of your musical past?"

"Well, I had memorized every piece of music needed for my advanced rudiments exam, and now I don't remember a single piece. But I'll relearn them. And I will pass the exam."

Dr. Fritz thought Garnet sounded awfully optimistic for someone in his shoes. "What about work? Do you have any idea when you might be reintegrated into the workforce, or when you might pick up your piano teaching, maybe get a full-time job?"

"The sooner the better," Garnet responded. "I want out of here as soon as possible."

"Well, at the rate you're going, it won't be long," Dr. Fritz said encouragingly.

They talked for about another half hour. Dr. Fritz briefly touched on the seizures and asked how he would feel living seizure-free.

"I feel like I've been born again, and am starting my life all over."

As he left, Dr. Fritz thought what a remarkable attitude this young man had. He doubted his patient would suffer any serious psychological scarring from the stroke but he also reminded himself it was too early to tell.

Chapter Twenty

Ella sat at her kitchen table, copying a picture of Michelle Pfeiffer from a magazine.

She also had many sketches of Pickles, her temperamental black cat, strewn across the kitchen table.

He sat on the couch next to her and eyed her suspiciously. His eyes darted back and forth, a guarded expression of caution and mistrust. He did not look relaxed. He seldom did.

The door rang and she answered it. She felt a sense of dread. Two volunteers from her church had arrived to clean her house. Sam and Linda had told her on the last visit that her place was an absolute pigsty and they had been sent from the church's community outreach program to fix it.

Ella hadn't liked their attitudes on the last visit, and she was sure this one wouldn't be much different. Sam had said if he told family services about the state of her townhouse she would have her child taken away and be declared an unfit mother.

Hardly an attitude for religious volunteers, Ella thought as she composed herself the best she could and opened the door for the pair.

"Did you do any of the things I told you to do?" Sam said, looking around. Linda busied herself by picking up clothes and other clutter on the floor.

Ella paused, trying to think of a response. "Do you guys say hello?" she finally asked.

"Fine. Hello, Ella," Sam said. "Did you do any of the things I told you to?"

"I cleaned out the bathroom and threw out some of the extra bottles. It looks better in there," Ella said.

Sam looked around the house disapprovingly as Pickles eyed the two intruders, his ears closing and his back arching in a predatory stance. He meowed loudly and darted into the kitchen, up on the counter, finally settling on top of the fridge, ready to attack. His eyes darted unblinkingly back and forth.

"Okay good," Sam said, and proceeded up the stairs to inspect the bathroom. Outside, thunder crackled and the hissing sound of rain began.

Pickles noticed the door open a crack. He leaped off the fridge and ran outside in the pouring rain. Ella ran after him, screaming.

The rain was coming down so hard she could barely see. She thought she saw a black ball dart across the alley, but she could not be sure.

"Pickles, Pickles, come," she called. But she couldn't hear or see anything. She walked down the entry laneway to her townhouse complex, calling out his name, her vision worsening. A little river of water ran down the lane, and she followed its splashing, knowing it would lead to the street and maybe to Pickles.

Thunder boomed and a flash of lightning cracked beside her, not ten feet away. She jumped in panic and started running. She saw a brief flash of light as she ran, and then heard a large thumping sound. The sound of her body bouncing off a car. She had run right into a moving vehicle in her panic and now sat on her butt in complete shock. She didn't know if she was okay, and felt a large welt beginning to form on her forehead.

An agitated bald man opened the door, jumped from the vehicle, and immediately started berating Ella. "What the fuck are you doing, you dumb bitch?" he said. "Are you fuckin' retarded or something? You ran right into the side of my car."

Instead of asking Ella if she was okay, he began inspecting the side of his vehicle for damage.

Ella felt the lump swell. She was stunned, probably mildly concussed, but thought she had better try and get to her feet. "Ugghhh," she said, struggling to her feet. "Pickles. I lost my cat. Back there. Scared. I ran. Uhhh, I'm sorry."

"You're stupid to look for a cat in this mess," the man said, still inspecting his vehicle. He seemed satisfied there was no damage. He opened the door, got in, and squealed his tires loudly, but not before flipping Ella the bird and telling her she would be better off locked in a padded room.

She stumbled to her feet, moving her hand up the goose egg on her forehead, gently massaging it. She turned in the direction of her townhouse and began staggering back. The second step she took she tripped over one of her feet and fell in the river of water with a loud splash.

As quickly as it had arrived, the rain began to let up, and she could see her unit in the distance.

She continued to call for Pickles as she opened the gate and walked into the small backyard. Pickles sat by the door under the protection of the porch awning and watched her nervously.

They were both drenched.

"There you are, my little sweetie," she said, scooping him up as she entered the unit.

"Where were you?" Sam asked. "You know we do this volunteer and could use a little help." He seemed oblivious to Ella's dishevelled, wet, and injured state. He started to say something else but then stopped. He noticed Ella's face was turning red.

"L ... Listen," Ella said. "And to do that you have to shut your mouth. My cat left the townhouse, I went looking for him, and I ran into a car. But, hey, I know that's something you couldn't care less about. All you care about is telling me what a mess my house is and that I will lose my daughter if family services ever found out."

Sam looked stunned. By this time, Linda had also appeared downstairs and was listening.

"Well, I've got news for you." Ella's voice was rising and Pickles had disappeared upstairs. He wanted no part of this.

"I want both of you out of my house now. Leave, go on! Go! If you don't think I can handle this on my own, just you wait and see."

Ella had a few more choice words in mind, but she realized she was wasting her breath. The two had taken their cue and left without saying a word.

What a bunch of religious hypocrites! She went upstairs to shower. The day was turning to evening and she still had an appointment to deal with.

Later, she sat in a church boardroom with the tech team, six volunteers who handled lighting and camera work for the orchestra performance. Normally, Garnet would be playing bass trombone or tuba, but on this day he obviously would not be part of the performance.

They would be performing for some elderly folk, and the tech team coordinator was briefing the team on what to do and how to arrange the lighting in sequence to the music.

The statuesque woman asked the group what they had done on the weekend. They all gave their stories.

Ella anxiously waited for her turn. In spite of the lump on her head and a slight kink in her neck, most of her body felt intact. She looked forward to telling them all about her husband's miraculous progress.

But when everyone had spoken, and Ella thought she would be next, the coordinator quickly starting giving lighting instructions. She ignored Ella altogether.

As the coordinator talked about camera angles and gave specific lighting instructions, Ella was devastated. It was as if she did not even exist. She fought to control the tears that were welling up inside her. When the tech team coordinator had finished, Ella ran to the church bathroom, isolated herself in a toilet stall, and began crying.

She called Debbie. She was not in the mindset to go through with her volunteer lighting job.

Debbie was on her way to a listing presentation when the phone rang. She was on another line, saw Ella's number come up, and told her client she would call him back.

"Hi Ella, how are you?" Debbie said in her usual cheerful voice.

Ella was sobbing. "I'm at my church. I haven't been having a very good day. I hate to ask this, but could you please come and get me? I don't feel that well."

Normally, Debbie would have hesitated, probably made some excuse, but this time she wanted to help.

"I'll be there in fifteen minutes, sweetie," she said, motioning Don to turn the vehicle around. On the way to the church, she called and rescheduled her appointment.

Thirty minutes later, Debbie and Ella sat in a coffee shop. Debbie did something she never did and left her phone in the car, instructing Don to forward the calls to her office.

Ella's tears had dried up now.

"People from church have decided to follow Christ, but they don't show a lot of compassion," Ella said. "People exclude me. I don't always go to church because of that. Why can't they imitate the attitude and actions of Jesus? They talk about wanting to follow Jesus, but it's all talk. They're hypocrites."

Debbie listened while Ella vented. Ella's phone rang. It was Sam, the volunteer house cleaner. He said Ella was not living up to her part of the bargain to keep the house clean and therefore there would be no more cleaning.

"Fine," Ella said, and hung up.

She explained the call to Debbie, claiming she was glad to be rid of the two.

"It's gross. I hate it. They were creepy," she said. "They think they can walk all over me and I should accept it because I don't have a lot of friends, because I look different."

"You have me," Debbie said soothingly, and held Ella's hand. "And you have a beautiful daughter. And you have Garnet."

"Thanks," Ella said, smiling slightly. She reached for a napkin and dabbed away a tear. "You're right. Lots of friends are detrimental anyway. Lots of people want to control a group, and if you're not towing the line, you're out. So many people are caught up in popularity nonsense and end up hurting people. They do more harm than good."

Debbie wondered about her quest to become Miss Popular and where it had gotten her. She thought she had lots of friends, and now began to wonder how many of them were really her friends. She had been stabbed in the back many times by people she had let into her inner circle, but she had no idea how it would be to go through life like Ella had to. Ella's story made her sad.

"According to Dr. Phil, that's a form of bullying," Ella said. "It's almost the same as the way girls do it in junior high. They talk about you behind your back, exclude you, want to see you alone. It's under-the-surface bullying; they can't outwardly show contempt, as it wouldn't look good."

"I never thought about it that way, but you have a point," Debbie said, trying to be positive.

"Well, yeah," Ella said, talking herself into a better mood. "You have to take it for what it is, though. When it happens, you have to overcome it. If you allow yourself to, you could get sucked under, and then it would be quite defeating."

Debbie wondered who was really providing the moral support. She felt encouraged by Ella's attitude, and the sadness slowly dissipated.

Chapter Twenty-One

It was coming up on three weeks now since Garnet's surgery. He had regained limited movement in the right side of his body. Doctors didn't know if he would ever fully recover full movement, but that didn't stop Garnet. He pressed on with his physiotherapy, determined to one day walk normally.

The right side of his face still felt numb, and he noticed his smile looked a little crooked. He only had limited movement in his right hand, and that bothered him because it meant he might not be able to play piano.

He was determined to try, however.

He studied for advanced rudiments in music, a critical course for music composition. He had completed his language and physiotherapy, talked to the hospital shrink, and now focused on his course.

Dr. Fritz walked into his room and greeted him. "Nice to see you're keeping busy," he said. Garnet dog-eared the page of his book as Dr. Fritz continued. "I forgot to tell you earlier, we have connections with a government-sponsored employment preparedness program and a life skills program that we want to see you enroll in."

"When does that start?" Garnet asked.

"In a week, at which time we feel you'll be ready for release."

Garnet's eyes lit up. He had anticipated a release, but he had no idea it would be this soon. "Excellent," he said. "I'm looking forward to getting back to my music and back to work."

"Good," Dr. Fritz said. "We have reduced the dosage on your anti-seizure medication, as by all accounts you should now be seizure-free for the rest of your life. We will continue to monitor you and monitor the dosage. If you are still seizure-free in another month, the dosage will be decreased again."

Garnet sighed. Despite the damage from the stroke, being seizure-free meant having a new beginning, one that would give him the freedom to pursue his dreams and goals. "Thanks," he said. "Thanks for telling me this. I look so forward to beginning a normal life."

Dr. Fritz knew it would be a long time before Garnet would see the day he would be living a normal life. He had diagnosed some brain function abnormality from the stroke, and he doubted Garnet's brain would ever fully repair itself. He suspected his patient's physical limitations would also be life-long.

But he wasn't one to rain on anybody's parade, and he admired Garnet's ambition and positive attitude. "Okay, great," he said. "One of our social workers will give you the details prior to your release. Good luck with your studies." Dr. Fritz left.

Garnet kept his book closed. He looked at his right hand, trying to move the fingers. They wiggled slightly. He guessed he probably had recovered 40% of his pre-stroke movement.

He opened and closed his fist as fast as he could, trying to will the 60% movement back. He did this until his hand ached, and noticed no noticeable change in movement. "It'll come back, don't you worry," he said to himself.

He planned on applying to Berklee College of Music in Boston, where he hoped to obtain a Bachelor of Fine Arts with a minor in composition and film scoring. From there, he planned on continuing to teach piano, do film scoring for the movies, and compose music.

His fingers ached from the exercise. He dismissed the pain, turning his attention to his newest composition, a piece entitled '61 Titles,' about his life and rebirth after the operation. The outline and the titles had come to him in his most recent dream.

He envisioned a grandiose musical production, replete with actors and a full orchestra. It would be performed by the church orchestra and would be months in the planning before it could finally be brought to full production.

Garnet also planned to submit it to Berklee to fulfill one of the pre-requisites he would need to be granted admission.

So much to do and not enough time to do it. He began to study for his advanced rudiments exam. "My life is really coming together," he said, and promptly fell asleep.

Chapter Twenty-Two

Ella slid down the playground slide and smiled as her friend Kristy waited for her at the bottom. "Wheeeee," she shouted as she reached the bottom, momentarily landing on her feet, and then falling forward.

Kristy grabbed her arm and steadied her. "No you don't," she said. "I won't let you fall."

"Your turn," Ella said, watching her ascend the ladder. "Put your feet and arms up in the air. You'll go faster."

Her friend complied, steadied herself on the slide with her elbows, and pushed off. Reaching the bottom, she jumped off, landing gracefully on her feet.

Nothing like Ella's uncoordinated attempt.

"Good run," Ella said, and hugged her friend.

Three girls approached from a distance. Kristy saw them and suddenly pushed Ella away.

"What's wrong?" Ella asked, and then noticed Kristy was looking at the three approaching girls.

Ella knew these girls. She also knew they didn't like her. They didn't like the way she looked, and had ridiculed her in the past, calling her "retard."

Kristy inched away from Ella as the girls approached.

As they neared, the tall one spoke first. "Kristy, come on, we're going over to Suzie's house. What do you want to hang around with a freak like that for?"

Ella winced.

Wrinkles creased Kristy's forehead as she made up her mind.

"I have to go," she said, and ran to her friends, who had already passed.

"No," Ella said, crying. "Come to my house and play with me."

It was too late. The image of the four girls grew smaller as they departed.

Ella crawled to the slide and pounded her head on it. It throbbed with pain. Small cuts opened up in her forehead, blood squirting down her head, into her eyes, nose, mouth, splattering her clothes, and staining the grey steel slide a shiny red.

"Noooooooo, noooooo, noooo, noo," she screamed with each thud.

She woke up, soaked in sweat, blankets and pillows in twisted disarray. She jerked up, realizing she had had a nightmare, one based on the rejection she suffered during her adolescence.

"Oh my God," she said, wiping the sweat from her brow, confirming it was just that.

Pickles sat in the corner of the room, his yellows eyes regarding her cautiously. He seemed frozen to the spot, unable or too afraid to move.

"Pickles, honey, it was just a dream—" A bolt of pain coursed through her temple and stopped the words immediately. Her head pounded. She slowly laid her head back on the one remaining pillow on the bed, hoping the pounding pain would subside.

What's wrong with me? she thought. She could not recall ever having a headache this painful.

Pickles, seemingly sensing danger, bolted from the room, meowing angrily as he left.

Ella remained on the bed, waiting, hoping, for the pain to subside. She thought about getting up to for a couple of Tylenol, but wasn't sure she was capable. She also felt dizzy, nauseous, and disconnected, like her brain was not processing information reasonably.

She strained to see a fly on the ceiling, and tried to focus on it to give her something to do, something to take her mind off the pain.

Her vision blurred and a fresh bolt of pain seared through her temple. Her stomach started churning and she felt like vomiting. The fly slowly crawled along the ceiling.

She could feel it coming. Her stomach was not buying the fly focus exercise. She felt a sudden wave of dizziness, could feel the vomit making its way up her esophagus. She tried to burp, to let the gas escape, but it didn't work. She tasted tangy puke.

The nausea intensified.

I have to get up. But wasn't sure if she could make it to the bathroom.

The puke rose in her throat.

I have to try. She made a desperate effort to get out of bed. She grabbed the end table to steady herself and tried to jerk herself up. The room started moving and she could see two doorways out of the bedroom. She was not sure which one was the real thing.

She ran for the open door, slammed into the wall, came crashing down on her back, and started vomiting as she lay there.

Wrong door.

I am going to choke on my own puke.

The yellow liquid flowed out of her mouth, down her pajama top, and onto the floor. She tried to stand again, determined to make it to the bathroom and clean herself up. She was still hacking as she stood up, and the vomit sprayed in several different directions as she made her second attempt at navigating the doorway.

She found the right exit, but as she rounded the corner to go into the bathroom, she slipped on the sticky trail of vomit, and careened down the stairs. She felt like she was floating, and everything was happening in slow motion.

She curled herself into a ball as she lurched into the air and bounced down the stairs. She heard the thuds as she descended, the cracking sound of bones breaking.

She crashed into the floor with a thud, kept rolling with the momentum, and slammed into the wall below. The snowball position of protection had uncurled somewhat, and by the time she reached the wall, she catapulted face first into it, arms outstretched.

Her body left an imprint on the wall.

Her head was wedged in the drywall. She tried to move. It hurt too much. She could not move a single limb. Her right leg was twisted back in an awkward position.

Everything went black and Ella wondered if this is what it felt like to die.

Chapter Twenty-Three

Susan's boyfriend pulled up in front of her house. She kissed him and stepped out of the car, noticing the moon was full and a few stars were out.

As she unlocked the front door, she was overcome by a feeling of unease. Something was wrong.

The feeling got worse as she stepped inside. She was overpowered by the stench of puke. She flicked the light on and walked in quickly.

She screamed when she saw her mother.

The upper part of Ella's body was embedded in the drywall. Her left leg was in a kneeling position on the outside of the wall and the right leg was pointing straight back. A pool of blood and sticky yellow liquid circled the scene.

Pickles stood beside Ella and meowed.

Susan called 911. "Help, help," she screamed when the dispatcher picked up. "My mom's fallen down the stairs. Her head's stuck in the wall."

"Is there a pulse?" the female dispatcher calmly asked.

"I, I, don't know."

"Could you go over and put your hand on her neck or wrist please?" the dispatcher asked in the same monotone voice.

Ella's head was embedded in the drywall, but a portion of her neck was exposed. Susan put her hand on it, and, in a panic stricken moment, thought she felt nothing. Then she pressed her thumb slightly deeper and did feel something.

A pulse.

She was alive. Susan sighed deeply.

"Yes, yes, I do feel something," she told the dispatcher.

"Good," the woman answered.

She told Susan to stay with her mother, not to attempt to move her, and that help would arrive within minutes.

Susan knelt down next to Ella and lightly stroked her arm.

Pickles, as if taking her cue, began licking Ella's other arm, taking care not to make contact with the gooey mess still oozing from the drywall and trickling down Ella's arms and back.

Audible groans came from behind the drywall. "Help me," Ella muttered as she slowly regained consciousness.

Startled, Pickles stopped licking and watched, wide-eyed.

"Mom, mom, you're alive," Susan declared.

"Aaaaaaaaaaaauuuugh," came the response. Ella opened her eyes and saw only blackness surrounding her. She smelled the puke and blood, and it dripped into her eyes.

She tried to move her right leg and it screamed in pain. Her groans turned into screams.

"Don't try and move, Mom," Susan said. "An ambulance is on its way."

Ella heard the words and they registered. The pain was too intense and she passed out again.

Chapter Twenty-Four

Garnet took a moment to soak in the morning sunlight before descending down the hospital stairs. He breathed in the fresh air, exhaled deeply, and smiled. "My new life," he said to himself. He looked around, trying to spot Susan or Ella.

He was sure they knew he would be released today, and wondered where they were.

His smile slowly faded as he scanned the bustling streets for his family. *Oh well. Nothing to do but head home and surprise them.* He felt a growing unease working its way up from the pit of his belly.

He looked down at his right leg, adjusted his walking stick (doctors had told him it was only temporary until he regained more motor control of his limbs) and took the first step down the stairs. He felt his right foot hit the next step, and as he lifted his left leg, he wobbled before steadying himself. His right leg did not yet have the strength he gave it credit for, and he stopped momentarily, took a couple of deep breaths, and waited until he felt confident enough to walk to the bus stop.

Dr. Fritz had offered to drive him home, after providing him details of the life skills and employment preparedness course he would be taking, but Garnet had politely refused. He wanted to be independent and was growing tired of being treated like an invalid.

He took the next step with more confidence and then stopped, wide-eyed.

Susan was running up the stairs in his direction.

He had seen that look on her face before, and he didn't like it. There was something terribly wrong.

"Daddy, Daddy, Mom fell down the stairs," Susan said gasping for breath as she reached him. "She's here in the hospital."

"Oh shit," Garnet said.

A few moments later the two were back inside the hospital waiting room, Garnet nervously sipping coffee and Susan eyeing the other people in the room. A man sat across from them, slumped over, his head in his hands. Occasionally, he would look up, sigh loudly, and then return to his slumped position. His face was wet, and Susan guessed he had been crying. She wondered what his situation was and instantly felt sorry for him.

Garnet looked pensive. *I can't seem to leave here. On the very day I'm supposed to be released, this happens. Of all the rotten luck.*

His daughter looked uncomfortable, so he put his arm around her. She managed a slight smile.

"Don't worry, honey," Garnet said. "Your mother will be fine. I know it."

About two hours later, though it seemed like an eternity to Garnet, Dr. Carsdale arrived.

"Ella is okay," he said in a low voice after sitting next to them. Susan and Garnet simultaneously breathed a sigh of relief.

"Ella is unconscious right now, in the operating room. She is still under anesthetic. She's actually lucky to be alive. She has a large cut on her forehead that required stitches. She also has a concussion from the fall. She broke her right leg in three places and we just finished operating to set it. It looks like it will be okay, but we'll have to see."

"Can we see her?" Susan asked.

"Not yet," Carsdale said. "She won't wake up for a few hours. It appears no other bones were broken, but there's something else you should know," Carsdale said. "We found a benign brain tumour that will have to be surgically removed. Not right away, but soon, as it is creating a lot of pressure inside Ella's head, making her dizzy and nauseous. We believe it caused the fall."

Garnet's mouth dropped open, the remaining color draining from his face. He went white as a sheet. "No, no, no," he said. "Not now, especially not now."

Carsdale put a hand on his shoulder, trying to calm him. "Take it easy. The prognosis for this type of tumour is very good, these tumours are rarely life threatening."

Susan assumed the slumped position of the man across from her, and began gently sobbing in her hands. The man looked up, a relieved expression on his face, as if he was happy that someone else was suffering.

Garnet put his hand on his daughter's shoulder again. He tried to muster more courage, a quality he now viewed as being in short supply. "I'm sure everything will be fine," he said, not at all convinced of the certainty of his words.

"Both of you should go home and get some rest," Carsdale said. "I'll call you when Ella wakes up. It's probably better to come back tomorrow. I'm sure she won't be in any shape to talk when she wakes, and she'll be in a lot of pain. She may also have trouble remembering things, at least in the short term."

On the bus ride home, Garnet and Susan were both preoccupied and didn't feel like talking. They sat with furrowed brows, oblivious to the buzz of traffic and conversations going on around them.

Chapter Twenty-Five

Ella did not know where she was.

She was cold. Freezing cold.

She tried to move, but her whole body ached. All she could see was black around her, and the air felt thick and damp, making it hard for her to breathe. She tried to open her mouth but nothing came out. She wanted to cry out for help.

Where am I?

She tried to move again but her body would not respond.

Then in a flash it came to her. She had fallen down the stairs at home. She vaguely remembered careening downward, thumping and thudding her way to the bottom, but couldn't remember anything at all after that. Point of reference. *What's my name?* She struggled for an answer, but none came. *What? I don't even know who I am? What's wrong with me?* She tried to bring herself back to the fall, to think about her house and who lived in it with her.

But all she remembered was the fall, nothing at all about her family.

Then a pair of yellow eyes came into focus in her mind's eye. Pickles. "I have a cat named Pickles," she said, her voice returning suddenly. That, she could remember. The thought comforted her, but only momentarily.

How can I exist like this? I must be dead. Dead and in hell. The thought horrified her, and she struggled to move her head.

Nothing.

She was in the bottom of a long, dark well. She strained to try and see a light. Perhaps there was one at the top of the well, and also a way out.

Then she saw it. Four glowing white dots, way up at the surface of the well.

What are the dots?

She tried to focus on them, noticing two were bunched together and the other two were slightly farther apart.

Like eyes.

Two dots moved a few inches and spoke. "Where were you last night?" She recognized the voice. It was her father, now dead. "Answer me. Where were you last night?"

Ella couldn't remember.

Then another voice. "Answer your father. Where were you last night?"

She knew that voice as well. It was her stepmother. They were interrogating her, like they had done so many years ago, when she was a child. She remembered that feeling only too well, how nervous she would become during the interrogations. How she couldn't remember.

I just remembered earlier. How come I can't remember now?

"Where was I last night?" she asked.

It seemed like this session would be no exception. Ella tried to remember. "Where was I last night?" she asked again, stalling.

"You can't even remember where you were last night?" her stepmother asked, her voice far away yet echoing down the well chamber.

"I'm trying," Ella said, a bead of perspiration forming on her forehead. "Give me a minute, will you?"

Her father spoke again. "Tell me where you were and what you were doing last night."

Ella couldn't remember.

Then, suddenly it did come to her, and a smile creased her lips. For once, she would be able to put them in their place, after so many years of drawing a blank.

"I was at home, sleeping. I had a headache. When I got up from my nap, I was dizzy and I felt sick. I fell down the stairs, must've hurt myself or ..." she trailed off. She didn't want to say the word. *If they're dead, and I'm talking to them, I must be dead.* She knew for sure her father was dead, but her stepmother, she wasn't sure. It had been so many years since she had had any contact with her.

A bead of sweat dripped down her head, rolled to the end of her nose, and lingered there. She tried to wipe it away and nothing happened. She felt another piercing stab of pain in her head as she concentrated, trying to get to the sweat droplet.

"Help me," she screamed up the well, now starting to panic. "Get me out of here!"

She tried to move her right hand. This time it did move, ever so slightly, and then stopped again. It felt like a leather restraint was blocking her movement.

"You've been a clumsy, stupid woman," her stepmother said, her voice distant but clear.

Then Ella noticed the eyes growing bigger, ever so slowly. And she could hear other voices ... or maybe it was the same voice.

"Ella, wake up. Wake up, please. Don't strain, you'll hurt yourself." The eyes grew bigger and the voices grew louder.

She opened her eyes to blinding light.

Dr. Carsdale and Janice stood over her bed, looking concerned.

"How are you feeling, Ella? Easy, easy there. Do you understand me?"

Ella tried to speak and her throat felt parched. "Yes, I do," she squeaked, noticing she was tied to the bed with leather restraints.

Her vision began to clear. Her right leg was suspended in traction and a large bandage was wrapped around her head. An IV was hooked into her arm, and a monitor beside the bed registered her vital signs.

Her head ached.

Her leg ached.

"We had to tie you down because after we stitched up your head and repaired your leg you started flailing around while you were still under," Carsdale said. "We didn't want you to hurt yourself."

"We can probably take them off now," Janice said.

He nodded and she began untying the straps. Ella's wrists were red and sore.

The nightmare about her parents and the black hole was still fresh in her mind and she remembered the bead of sweat. She felt it still clinging to her nose. Janice noticed it as well and wiped her face with a warm damp cloth.

"How do you feel?" Carsdale asked.

"Uhh, tired and sore. I have a headache."

"How many fingers am I holding up?"

"Three."

"Right. Now?"

"Six."

"Right. And one more time."

"Four."

"Good," Carsdale said. "Actually, you are very lucky to be alive, young lady. You put a large gash in your forehead requiring thirty-six stitches, and broke your leg in three places. We had to screw some of the bones in place to put you back together. But it should heal up nicely." Carsdale cleared his throat and continued. "You have a concussion from the fall. And, during the brain scan, something else came up."

"Something else?" Ella asked, trying to shake the cobwebs from her head. Along with her pain, she still felt dizzy from the anesthetic and a little high from what she suspected was a morphine drip going into her right forearm.

"We found a brain tumour."

Ella's mouth dropped open.

"Don't worry, it's benign and totally operable. We want to keep you here a few weeks to monitor your concussion, release you for about a month so you can heal, and then schedule a craniotomy, an operation to remove the tumour."

"That would explain the dizziness and headaches I've been having," Ella said. "I think that caused my fall."

"I think you're right. Now, I'll have more questions for you later, but I think it's important right now you get some rest." He left the room.

Janice lingered and adjusted Ella's pillows, both on her head and on her mending right leg. She gave Ella a glass of water, gently holding it to her mouth while Ella drained it. Her throat felt awfully parched, and the cold water was refreshing.

"Where are Garnet and Susan?" Ella finally asked.

"They were here earlier but they went home. You were still unconscious. Garnet has been released from the hospital and he's home with your daughter right now. I'm sure they'll be in tomorrow."

Garnet fidgeted with his computer as he thought about his wife. Pickles watched him quizzically, seemingly surprised to see his face in the house after such a long absence.

Garnet was annoyed his right hand would not do what he wanted it to, but plugged away on the keyboards, undaunted. He woke from a fitful sleep, worried about Ella, and could not get back to sleep. So he got up and started on his 61 Titles.

His left hand typed okay, but the right was not yet coordinated enough, and he was all thumbs and forefinger. His hand jerked, killing the power to the laptop. The computer powered down, erasing his last hour of work.

Annoyed, he rebooted it.

It was 3:45am and Susan was fast asleep. Pickles, however, seemed curious to see how the reboot would go.

"Bloody hand," Garnet said and pounded it on the desk, as if punishing it would somehow make it work better. "Ouch," he said emphatically. Pickles had heard enough and bolted under the couch, a whining meow trailing his exit.

The computer beeped back to life and he continued. He typed the first title, "Fearfully And Wonderfully Made," and started hack-typing the musical notes for the intro, wincing as he tried to will his right hand to do what it absolutely didn't want to do.

He finished some notes and wiped his brow, realizing he was sweating.

He took a moment to save the material before continuing. As he typed, his eyes began to close, and soon he was fast asleep at the keyboard.

Chapter Twenty-Six

"I'm Chaddie," the man said to Garnet, extending his hand. Garnet was eating an egg salad sandwich, holding it in his left hand. He tried to extend his right hand to greet the man but it wouldn't work. He put down the sandwich and extended his left hand.

Chaddie switched hands and shook his. "My name is actually Chad, but everyone always calls me Chaddie, which I've gotten used to."

Garnet wondered if the man, who was in his 50's with brown hair and a roughly trimmed goatee, was saying "Chattie," but thought better than to ask.

"Nice to meet you. I'm Garnet."

It had been two days since Ella's admission to the hospital. Garnet was at his employment course, on his lunch break.

Garnet and Susan had been up both days to visit Ella, who seemed to be doing well, considering. While her memory was a little foggy on a few things, and doctors wanted to monitor her concussion for another week or two before releasing her, she seemed to have adjusted remarkably well to her impending surgery, and her spirits were up.

Chaddie took a seat next to Garnet in the cafeteria of the government facility and started telling his life story, although Garnet hadn't asked to hear it.

Chaddie drank frequently and abundantly, almost every day by his own admission, and lived with his mother. He was mechanically-inclined and loved to tinker with automobiles, occasionally earning the odd dollar working on friend's vehicles. Most of the money he earned went to alcohol.

He was a highly-trained martial artist and boxer. Beneath this surly exterior, Chaddie was friendly and approachable, and it wasn't long before he and Garnet were exchanging stories, making jokes, and commenting on the course.

"My mother wanted me to do something with my life," Chaddie said, and paused. He looked bewildered for a moment, and then offered, "I guess she thinks I need a career or something." He paused again, then continued. "I have no clue what I want to do with my life. You?"

Garnet told him a few things about his life, then added, "That's what this course is all about. Maybe it will help."

"Yeah, maybe," Chaddie said.

It was time to return. Garnet, with his new cane, limped alongside Chaddie as they re-entered the room. Chaddie relocated to a vacant spot right beside Garnet.

Once the twelve students were seated, Coach Michael began. "I want to continue with resumé preparation," he said. He was a bald, beefy man who grinned often as he talked. "In today's competitive job market, it's critical that you have a professional and presentable resumé." He began handing out sample resumés. "Take these samples and have a look at them. One is a chronological resumé, and the other highlights specific accomplishments, probably more suited to a professional or a person who has had long gaps in their employment history. Remember, your resumé contains much more than a chronology of jobs. It is also an advertisement for you, highlighting your other accomplishments and skills."

As Michael talked, Garnet looked around the classroom, noticing that Chaddie had his eyes on the legs of a particularly stunning blonde seated at the front.

Garnet couldn't help noticing her earlier in the day, as her low cut skirt displayed perfect legs and her blouse revealed magnificent cleavage and an ample bosom. He wondered how a beautiful woman like her could possibly benefit from a course like this.

He re-focused on the resumé sample as Chaddie caught his eye, smiled, and winked.

"What resumé do you think you would best benefit from?" Michael asked, addressing Chaddie.

Chaddie looked confused. He picked up the sample resumés. "Um ... I've had some dry spells in my jobs," he responded after a long pause.

"So, would you want the chronological or the achievement resumé then?" Michael asked.

"The achievement, I guess," he finally said. "But I haven't achieved a lot lately."

This drew a burst of laughter from the class. When the laughter subsided, Michael continued. "Well, if you're clever, you can certainly hide the gaps in your employment by highlighting your achievements. And, if you haven't achieved a lot, as you say, get out there and achieve, even if you have to start volunteering. What are you good at, Chad?"

"I'm Chaddie."

"You like to talk. Okay, well, that can be useful in sales."

"No, my friends call me Chaddie."

"Oh, sorry." The class laughed some more. "Okay, Chaddie, what are you good at, and what do you like to do?"

"Well ... I'm pretty good with a hammer. And carpentry. And I can fix cars."

"Do you fix cars now as a hobby?"

"Yeah, I do. We have a big shop at the back of the house and I work on cars there sometimes."

"Well, there you go. That hobby would be an excellent lead into auto mechanics. Put it in your resumé."

A flicker of excitement flashed across Chaddie's face.

At the end of the class, Michael prescribed a rather unusual homework assignment. "Write a poem about what you think this course is all about," he told the students.

On the bus enroute to the hospital, Garnet thought about the assignment. *Maybe Michael wanted to determine if there were any creative students in the class, who might benefit from some specialized training?*

As the bus rolled along, Garnet wrote in his notebook. Occasionally he looked out at the sunlight reflecting off the red and yellow leaves. It was now October, and although the days had been sunny, the leaves had started to change color and fall, and the weather was becoming colder.

By the time he arrived, dusk was taking hold. The sky looked grey, the temperature far colder than it had been only an hour and a half before. Before exiting the bus, Garnet looked at his poem, mouthing the words to himself.

There was a coach who had a class

Of this he sure was proud.

Twelve students made up this great mass,

Each one spoke right out loud.

Every student, big and tall, had a different point of view.
This helped the course to spread ideas,
And come up with something new.
One thing, however, this class had learned,
Was help your fellow man.
For in this way, you live your life,
The best way that you can.
Satisfied, Garnet disembarked.

In Ella's room, he wasn't feeling so satisfied. She had had a bad day. Her leg was giving her a lot of pain, and the pain in her head had intensified. Garnet looked down at her. Her head still sported a massive bandage, her right leg was up in traction, and she had two black eyes, the result of the collision with the wall. Her hair was dishevelled. She winced when she spoke and sometimes her sentences made no sense.

Garnet wondered how the concussion might have affected her already short-term memory loss. He had a sinking feeling in his stomach.

She needed him, needed him to start making money now.

"Couldn't eat breakfast this morning. Puked it all up, all over the linens. Couldn't eat it at all. They changed the linens, tweaking my leg in the process. Now it's raging in pain," Ella explained. "Then the guy next to me"—she motioned to the empty bed beside her, separated only by a fabric wall partition—"goes and dies. Yeah, lets out one thundering scream, then nothing. Dead. Full medical team in here, and they couldn't revive him. Oh, and did I tell you I couldn't eat my breakfast?"

"Yes, honey, you did." Garnet gently kissed her on the cheek.

She looked at him with tears welling in her eyes. "I'm sorry for complaining so much. I must sound like a broken record. I just want to get out of here."

Garnet gently caressed her forehead.

"It's going to be okay," he said. "You're going to recover, get out of here, have a successful surgery, and everything will be fine. I'm going to start looking for work tomorrow."

Ella forced a smile.

"I started my employment course today, honey," Garnet said. "I'm learning resumé preparation. I really enjoyed the class." He wiped a tear from her eye with a tissue as he continued. "I wrote a poem today. Look."

Ella read the paper. She smiled, this time her full and unnaturally crooked smile. "You're so creative, dear."

Leaving the hospital, he didn't feel all that creative anymore. Ella's plight had darkened his spirits.

He bumped into an old friend in the corridor, and his smile returned. It was Lenny, whom Garnet had worked for when he first came to Calgary. Lenny owned an auto body shop, and Garnet would come in once a month to clean the little office, spray down the shop, and wipe all the walls.

Lenny was drunk and had a large cut on his forearm that was bleeding all over the floor. Although he had his hand over it, covering most of the gash, blood still oozed out.

"Lenny," Garnet said, concerned.

"Garnet, how the hell are you? I'd shake your hand, but I had a little trouble with a beer bottle."

Garnet limped over to Lenny, putting his arm on his shoulder. "Look, friend, emergency is that way, you want to go and have that looked at." He turned Lenny around and began escorting him to emergency.

In his time at the hospital, he had come to know it very well.

"How the hell are ya?" Lenny asked again as they walked down the corridor.

"I'm okay," Garnet said, though he wasn't feeling so okay at that moment.

"You married?" Lenny asked.

"Yes, I was just visiting my wife. She had a little accident."

"Oh, hope she's okay."

"I think she will be."

"Jesus, it's been a while since I've seen you, Garnet. We go back such a long time. We're old, you know, you and me."

"I'm not that old, Lenny, but when you hired me years ago, I was just a young kid, remember?"

"We go way back," Lenny said. "School days, remember?"

Garnet didn't remember because it wasn't true. He had never gone to school with Lenny. And he was about fifteen years younger than him.

"You hired me," he tried.

"We're fuckin' old, you and I. You know I'm sixty now. You must be the same, Garnet."

"Age is just a number in your mind," Garnet said.

"You're right. I can be as old or as young as anybody wants me to. I know I don't look my age. How old do I look, Garnet?"

"Fifty, maybe, but definitely not sixty," Garnet lied.

"You married?" Lenny asked again. "I went through an ugly divorce a few years ago and I'm single."

"You still in the auto body business?" Garnet asked.

"Thirty five years," Lenny said. "Pays the bills. You know, my divorce was ugly and it didn't have to be. What's with women, anyway? Rake you over the coals emotionally and financially."

Garnet only nodded, and Lenny continued his rant.

"I don't think I'm all bad-looking, do you, Garnet? I'm drunk right now, I know, but I still ain't bad-looking, am I?"

"No, you're not bad-looking, Lenny."

"Then why the fuck am I so lonely? I don't have a girlfriend, haven't in years. You know what I do? I wander around the streets at night by myself, go to different bars. I meet lots of women, lots of really young ones even, and they say I look young, I look great, even the older ones say that, but they never go home with me. So, yes, I'm very lonely and I'm trying to find a woman. But I can't, Garnet. They never come home with me."

Lenny staggered into an empty stretcher, sending it careening down the hall. Garnet, limping beside him, steadied his friend.

"Easy, Lenny, we're almost there."

They were almost at the rear entrance to the emergency ward when a nurse noticed the pair, and Lenny's injury, and took him by the other arm.

"Come this way, sir, let's get that looked at right away."

"Why won't they come home with me, Garnet? What's wrong with me?"

"You take care, Lenny," Garnet said, releasing his grip. "Don't worry, you'll find someone."

"Great to see you, Garnet," Lenny said. "I hope to see you again."

"Me too," Garnet said. The nurse escorted Lenny through the automatic sliding doors into the emergency room.

As he limped on, Garnet thought about how much Lenny had changed. When Garnet had worked for him, he was so positive, always socializing with lots of attractive women, and the world indeed seemed to be his oyster. Now, he had become a bitter, lonely drunk.

In spite of himself, Garnet smiled. Maybe, just maybe, his situation wasn't all that bad after all. Here was a man who had everything. Lots of women. Lots of toys. Lots of friends. And now he was reduced to wandering the streets by himself, without any friends, in search of the one thing Garnet had.

Love.

Chapter Twenty-Seven

The diminutive Asian man was in an absolute fury—a fury that belied his small stature. He stormed out of the back porch entrance, stopped, and flung the green garbage bag in the air. It landed with a crash. He yelled at Susan in Cantonese before returning to the townhouse.

Susan assumed he'd screamed some profanity, but she couldn't understand Cantonese, so she only winced at the words, and tightened her grip on Pickles, whose claws were now beginning to pierce through her clothing.

"Easy, Pickles," she said, attempting to loosen his death-grip on her forearm. She gently massaged his paws and he loosened his grip, letting out a high-pitched meow.

Jun had arrived about an hour ago and promptly told Susan to get out of the house. She protested briefly, but when he produced the eviction order, she went outside.

He appeared on the back porch again with another green garbage bag and flung it into the lawn. It landed with a gentle thump. *This one must contain clothing*, Susan thought.

A few curious neighbours stood outside, watching the entertainment. The backyard was beginning to fill with garbage bags and furniture.

Susan watched unhappily. A tear rolled down her cheek and she quickly wiped it away, determined not to let the people around her see how upset she was. *Where are we going to go? What are we going to do?*

She remembered that Debbie had loaned the family some money, but she didn't have a clue what her mom had done with it. Now Ella was in the hospital and Garnet was out of work. How were they going to pay the rent?

Jun appeared again and flung a kitchen chair on the lawn.

Her drunk neighbour Frank watched the whole thing, becoming angrier by the second.

"What the fuck are you doin', man?" he yelled at Jun. "You can't do that with people's shit, man. You have to' give 'em time to take it."

Jun wasn't impressed at the intrusion. He was about to yell something back, then, noticing Frank's ample bulk, decided to tone down his response. He wasn't up for a physical battle with a slobbering drunk.

"You mine own business," he said. "They don' pay rent an' they live like pigs. I come back with sheriff," he added, hoping the mention of an authority figure would tune this drunken slob up.

Unfortunately for Jun, he had picked the wrong tact. Frank hated the law and hated any mention of the police.

Jun turned to go inside again. He was startled by a smashing sound. Frank had hurled his beer bottle at the little Asian.

If Jun hadn't turned when he did, the bottle would have hit him square in the head. Instead, it narrowly missed him and smashed through the screen door window, sending shards of glass flying.

Jun opened his mouth to say something, but Frank had already left his little backyard and was walking toward Jun, fists clenched, ready for war.

"You get the fuck outta here, you little fuckin' puke. That ain't right what yer doin."

Jun ran into the house, slamming and locking the storm door behind him.

Frank kept advancing and Susan had to sidestep him to avoid a collision. Pickles was quiet, his yellow eyes focused on the drama.

"Done worry, honey," Frank said, staggering past Susan. "That fucker needs to give ya time to git yer shit. An' I'll make damn sure he does."

Susan managed a weak smile, deciding it was better to keep her mouth shut. After all, she was starting to feel the cold bite of winter as dusk took hold and the temperature dropped. It would be nice to warm up a bit.

Frank was on a mission. He walked up the porch, pulled back the broken screen door, and kicked open the main door, shattering bits of wood in the process. The door flung open, the force of the blow sending Jun flying across the room.

Frank advanced on him, a glazed, angry look in his eyes. "You git the fuck outta here, little man," he said, picking Jun up in the air with both hands

"Put me down, put me down," Jun screamed. "I call cop." Jun pounded on Frank's back with his little fists as he was being carried. The blows had little effect.

"Go ahead and call the fuckin' cops, ya little shit," Frank said as he carried Jun to the front door. "An' I'll tell 'em ya didn't give these nice folks here the proper notice before kickin' 'em out. You can't do that, ya little shit."

He carried Jun out onto the front porch, put him down, and kicked him in the ass, sending him toppling off the porch and landing in the strewn out debris.

"There, how d'ya like that? You think you can throw people's shit around like that? How does it feel to get thrown around like a piece of trash yerself?"

Jun slowly picked himself up from the pile of junk. He ran toward his yellow SUV, thinking this crazed maniac was not yet done with him. "I call cop," he said as he opened his driver door to get in. "I charge you with violence."

"Look, you little fuck," Frank responded. "I don't want to see ya here fer at least another forty-eight hours, so these nice folks here have time to clear their shit outta yer property. Do I make myself clear?"

Jun hesitated, perhaps thinking better of encouraging any future confrontations with his next-door neighbour. Who knew what this ape was capable of? He looked at Susan. "Two days, you not gone, I come back with sheriff, you hear me?"

Susan nodded. Pickles, sensing his moment, bolted from her grasp, raced up the walkway, and into the open door of the townhouse.

Jun drove away.

"Told ya I'd take care of that little shit," Frank said, and went inside his house before Susan could thank him.

The people who had been watching slowly began filtering back into their homes, their excitement for the day over for now.

Susan went inside the house retrieved a broom, garbage bag, and dustpan, and cleaned the broken glass.

No point in calling her dad, as she knew his cell phone had recently been disconnected. Arrears.

And her mom didn't have the money for a hospital land line.

She finally picked up the landline. No dial tone. She assumed it had also been disconnected due to arrears.

She remembered her pay-as-you-go cell phone and went to retrieve it in the kitchen drawer. It wasn't there. The entire contents of the drawer had been emptied into a garbage bag and tossed onto the lawn.

She sat down on the only kitchen chair left in the house began to cry softly.

Who was she going to call, anyway? Maybe her boyfriend Hank, but what could he do? The last time she had talked to him, his car wasn't running and he had been fired from his job.

"My life sucks," she said to no one in particular.

Pickles emerged from underneath the couch and meowed softly, vying for her attention.

Garnet stood outside in shock, viewing the mounds of debris piled up in his yard.

"What the heck happened?" he asked, limping up the porch steps.

His daughter was hunched over one of the bags with a flashlight, examining its contents.

"Susan, honey, what happened?"

"We've been evicted," she said, looking up. "Jun kicked me out and dumped a bunch of stuff on the lawn before Frank came and threw him out."

Garnet's jaw dropped.

Suddenly, for no apparent reason, Susan burst out laughing.

Her father had his arm around her. "What's so funny?"

"Would you rather I cried?"

Garnet stared at her for a moment, and then he started laughing as well. Soon the two of them were laughing uncontrollably. A few of the neighbours' porch lights came on, and one nosy neighbour, old Miss Higgins, even stepped outside, probably to see if she could acquire a ringside ticket for round two, David versus Goliath.

But once she saw there was no misery to enjoy, she quickly retreated inside her house.

The two stopped laughing. Garnet went inside and left his daughter searching for her cell phone. He tried to think of who he could call to help them out. The only person who came to mind was his drunkard uncle Bob, who lived in Martindale with his crotchety wife Helen. At least Bob had a pick-up truck, a garage, and an extra bedroom for Susan. Garnet would have to sleep on the couch.

Susan walked into the kitchen with the cell phone and handed it to him. "Any ideas?" she asked.

"I was thinking of Bob," Garnet said.

"No, no, I don't want to go there. He has a yappy poodle, an ornery wife, and he drinks like a fish. And he hates cats. What about Pickles?"

"It's only temporary until we can get on our feet, honey. I'm going to look for work tomorrow. Maybe you can find a part-time job, too?"

Susan liked the idea. And her family certainly needed the money.

"I don't even know if he'll take us, sweetie, but I should try. Don't you think?"

"Don't we have any more friends, Dad?"

Garnet couldn't think of any. Debbie had been particularly good to them lately and he didn't want to push the envelope. He really was in a pickle.

At least Bob was family. He dialed his uncle's number.

"Whaaaat?" Bob answered in his gruff voice. "Turn that goddamned thing down," he said to someone in the room, and the background music faded.

"Bob, it's me, Garnet."

"What do you want?" Bob wasn't one for small talk. "What are you calling me this late for?"

It was about nine. He heard the background music rise again and then Bob's voice. "I said turn that goddamned thing down! Can't you see I'm on the phone?" The music faded.

Garnet suspected Bob and Helen were both drunk, and Helen was egging her husband on, as she often did. It seemed the two had a power struggle that alcohol only exacerbated.

"Listen, Bob, I need a place to stay. Only for a week or two until I can get on my feet. We've been evicted. I have forty-eight hours to clear my stuff out."

The other end of the receiver was silent for a long moment. Susan stared at her father. Pickles had now moved to a position on the couch and his yellow eyes watched Garnet.

"I'll bring my pick-up truck over tomorrow evening," Bob said. "Make sure you have your shit packed. And what I decide is not worth taking stays in that fuckin' house, you got that?"

Garnet started to thank his uncle, but the phone went dead. Bob had hung up on him.

He smiled at his daughter. "Looks like we have a place to stay."

Chapter Twenty-Eight

Susan stood outside the McDonald's close to her home. It was nine in the morning and large snowflakes drifted around her. The wind howled and she shivered.

She walked toward the entrance, determined to get a job application. Geoff, Miss Higgins' teenage son, bumped her on the way in. He was with one of his motley-looking friends.

"Getting kicked out, are you?" Geoff said. "The retards are finally leaving," he told his buck-toothed friend with the baseball cap. Both of them snickered. "We don't need retards in our complex anyway," Geoff said and laughed.

"Then what are you doing there?" Susan asked, picking up her pace and reaching the entrance.

"You fuck off and go to hell," she heard him say as she closed the door. She wondered if he would follow her, but when she glanced back, she noticed they were walking away.

Susan swallowed the lump in her throat and stood in line.

Garnet pounded the pavement of Stephen Avenue, a street in Calgary that was dotted with a mix of high-end stores, pubs, restaurants, and a few retail shops of a seedier variety. The seedier businesses gave the street a bit of an identity crisis.

He had walked into six businesses so far and had been rejected by all of them. A few store employees had given him applications, claiming the boss wasn't around and he should come back another time.

He now stood outside of a small but clean-looking business called Bud's Barber Shop. Its exterior sported the traditional red and white colors.

A pink neon sign in the window proclaimed the store OPEN. Garnet read the black and white sign that also displayed prices. Men's Haircut $20, Shave $10, Shave and Haircut $25, Women's Haircut and Styling $35, Color $25, Shoeshine $7. Garnet looked in the window and noticed it was full of customers. At least two of the men seemed to be getting haircuts, the third a shave. His face was lathered thick, and an older black man worked on him with a straight razor.

Garnet could see another dusty leather chair in the back of the store. It was empty. There were no mirrors around it. Nothing but a wooden box containing shoe-shine accoutrements.

One of the patrons became impatient, said something to the black man, and left.

Garnet entered the shop just as the impatient man was leaving.

Chapter Twenty-Nine

Ella walked through a dark forest. Everything was black and she was shivering in the cold. What guided her now were the bright white stars illuminating the sky, vaguely pointing to the weaving trail up ahead.

She had become lost in the forest and was now looking for refuge, a place to warm up. She tripped over a small log outcrop and stumbled, hitting her head on a nearby maple tree. She rubbed the bruise on her forehead and it ached.

Her right leg and her head thudded in pain as she trudged along the trail. She didn't know how she had become lost in this forest, where it was, or when, for that matter, she had been released from hospital. *The result of poor short-term memory,* she thought.

She heard a high-pitched whistling sound in the woods ahead. It came again, a little closer this time. Her leg ached but carried her along. It must have healed all right.

Ahead, she saw an illuminated grey mist surrounding a clearing in the distance. As she got nearer, the light became brighter and she saw the outline of a house.

She sighed, hoping she could warm up and get some directions. As she reached the clearing, she noticed an illuminated sign fastened to the porch of the old, dilapidated house.

It read, "Fantasma Retreat Centre."

She walked down the winding pathway to the front door. The misty light surrounding the house seemed unnatural. The branches of the old apple tree on the front lawn arched in many different directions, some of them drooping dangerously low and close to the winding entry path. Ella sidestepped a branch that threatened to hook her thin jacket.

She crossed her fingers and walked up the rickety steps onto the porch. Knocked on the door.

Didn't hear a sound.

Her heartbeat quickened. The door flew open and a tall, grey-bearded man eyed her curiously. "What can I do for you?"

Ella jumped at the sight of him. More than his beard was grey. His raggedy clothes, dishevelled hair, and gaunt face were also grey. He looked like a ghost. She had to force herself to stay motionless for fear of running off into the forest in a panic. *Can't do that. Need to warm up.*

"Uhh, I'm lost. And cold."

"Oh, we're all lost in this house," the man replied. "Come in out of the cold." He opened the door and Ella walked into the dark, candlelit house.

She stopped in the living room and smiled. A wood-burning fireplace roared, two rocking chairs perched nearby it, and chopped wood was stacked to the ceiling. The house smelled damp and musty, but the fireplace looked inviting.

The man gestured for her to have seat, and she sat in one of the rocking chairs, holding her hands out toward the fire to warm them.

"My name's Earl," the man said. "Would you like some hot tea?"

"I'm Ella. Yes, that would be nice."

He returned with some tea and handed it to Ella. She took the tea, noticing that when she touched his hand, her fingers seemed to go right through it. This frightened her, and she jerked back, spilling some of the hot liquid on her pants.

"No need to be afraid," Earl said. "This is a retreat centre. You'll be safe here."

"Where am I?"

"You're in the Foothills Hospital, in a coma."

"I'm what?" Ella asked, the color draining from her features.

"I think you heard me," Earl began. "It looks like you fell asleep after your concussion and slipped into a coma. This is a retreat of sorts. You can recover here or you can die here, it all depends on you."

"I don't want to die," Ella said nervously, sipping the hot tea. It tasted good, bittersweet, and it warmed her insides.

"Nobody wants to die. But it's something we must all embrace because it will happen to all of us. Our life is finite. That's one of the few things we can be sure about."

"So, you're not real then?"

"I'm a ghost. I look after this house, take care of the guests and some of the more permanent residents. I'll tell you my story sometime, but not now. You're not ready yet."

She looked around the house, noticing one of the bedroom doors was slightly ajar. She thought she heard the same whistling sound coming from the room, but this time much fainter and with a kind of musical quality to it. At least it didn't sound threatening anymore. But she felt scared. She felt her arm and it felt solid enough.

"It's up to me, then, if I live or die?"

"Yes."

"Well, I want to live. I want to wake up."

"That's not entirely up to me, you see," Earl pointed out, rubbing his thick beard contemplatively. "You have to fight if you want out of here. Not me, of course, and not any of the clients. It's an inner fight. You have to prove your will to live to the eye in the sky."

"What, you mean God?"

"I've never been a particularly religious person, so I just refer to the higher power as the eye in the sky. But yes, something like that, I guess."

"So what do I do now?"

"There's lots of time for that," Earl said. "You have to understand you're in a transitional space right now, somewhere between life and death, caught in the middle. Whether you make it out of here will depend on your will to live. You'll have to fight for your survival, and you will be tested."

"Tell me what you want me to do."

"Plenty of time, my dear. For now, you should sleep."

Ella felt tired. Maybe it was chronic fatigue syndrome, one of the ailments she had suffered over the years. She wondered if she could be plagued by this ailment in a coma. She didn't understand anything too well right now.

Chapter Thirty

Garnet walked, or rather limped, into Bud's Barber Shop and a few heads looked in his direction.

"Are you Bud?" he asked the black man shaving a customer.

"I am," the man said, and smiled. "What can I do for you, young man?"

"Sorry to disturb you, but I'm looking for work."

Bud expertly glided the straight razor over his customer's neck, tipped off the foam into a nearby sink, and eyed Garnet curiously. He noticed Garnet's limp, the contorted side of his face, and the way he held his arm curled stiffly in front of him.

"What can you do? Can you cut hair?"

"No ... I just got out of the hospital from brain surgery, so I'm still recovering. But I can shine shoes." Garnet pointed to the dusty shoeshine chair in the corner of the room. "Doesn't look like that's been used in a while."

Bud resumed his work with the straight razor. His bald customer had a rather perturbed expression, perhaps unhappy at the intrusion, or maybe worried that Bud might have problems multi-tasking.

Before Bud could say anything, Garnet added, "Can I come back tomorrow when you're less busy and talk to you?"

A long pause. "Sure, can you come in at eight-thirty in the morning? I open at nine, so that should give use some time to talk."

"See you then," Garnet said, and left the shop before Bud had a chance to change his mind.

As he sat on the bus heading home to pack his belongings, Garnet was absolutely beaming about the possibility that he might soon become a shoe-shine boy.

That changed the following afternoon, however.

"She's in a what?" he asked Dr. Carsdale. He sat beside his jaundiced wife, who was lying lifeless on her hospital bed.

"She fell into a coma in her sleep last night," Carsdale explained gently. "We think it was triggered by her fall. But we have to be patient. We did another brain scan this morning and found the tumour seems to be unaffected by the fall. It hasn't gotten any worse since the coma. Sometimes these things happen, and she may snap out of it in a day or so."

"And what if she doesn't?" Susan asked.

"I think it's a little early to go into that right now," Carsdale said, "particularly in light of the recent trauma you've both been through."

Garnet didn't know what to say. He stared at his wife.

After his interview with Bud, he had met Bob and Susan at their townhouse, packed their belongings into his pick-up truck, along with some help from neighbours and a rather intoxicated friend of Bob's, and moved some things into Bob's house and garage.

Bob had insisted they leave a number of furniture articles behind, claiming he did not have the space to store them nor the where-with-all to try to sell them. Sarah and Pickles had slept in the spare bedroom, and Garnet spent the night on Bob's couch, listening to Helen and Bob argue drunkenly in the kitchen. He heard Helen refer to his family as "that fuckin' Garnet, that stupid cat, and that goddamned Susan brat."

Not exactly the red carpet treatment.

Garnet was determined leave as soon as possible.

The good news was Bud hired him that morning and Susan had also gotten a job at McDonald's. After work, the two had rushed up to visit Ella and tell her the good news, only to be disappointed by the news of her current condition.

Garnet thought he saw his wife's eyes fluttering. Yes, he did see them flutter. "What's with that?" he asked Carsdale. "She's moving. Ella, honey, can you hear me?" he said.

Nothing.

"Ella, Ella, speak to me. Nod if you can hear me. Extend your right index finger if you can hear me."

Ella remained motionless, and even her eyes stopped fluttering. The monitors beeped in rhythm to her steady heartbeat.

Carsdale watched patiently as Garnet attempted to snap Ella out of her coma. Finally, he said, "Why don't you go home and get some rest, both of you."

About a half hour later, Susan and Garnet sat on the bus on their way to Bob's house. Their expressions were both grim. They said nothing. They were not looking forward to another night with Bob, Helen, and the yappy poodle Muskeg.

Chapter Thirty-One

"They tried leasing it themselves for two months and couldn't do it," Brad said to Debbie. "Two months of lost revenue, I felt bad for them. Then I stepped in, called some of my solid contacts, had it leased in a week. That's how good I am." He stopped only momentarily to sip his coffee before continuing.

By this time, Debbie had almost completely tuned him out, only glancing occasionally between sips of her tea and nodding at the appropriate times. That was all it took to keep Brad ranting on.

He was relaying a story about how he had helped his clients buy a downtown condo. They tried to lease it on their own, given up, and hired Brad to take over. She had heard the story previously and knew that he had lucked out on the rental ad, as it had connected him to an agent who leased properties for some big oil companies in the city.

The agent, as it turned out, had a steady stream of imports to the city who were only too happy to pay $1,500 a month for a downtown two-bedroom condo in the sky. After all, they could walk to work and on their salaries, easily afford the rent.

As they sat in The Second Cup coffee shop on busy Macleod Trail, Debbie wondered about her friend's propensity for bullshit. Didn't he even remember telling her the story before, only last time mentioning the oilfield leasing agent as a stroke of luck?

Brad was a loyal friend who would give her the shirt off his back (not that she would want it) if she were ever in trouble financially, but she had no idea what made him bullshit and brag so much. When she was with him, she would often just tune him out and think about other things. Now, she wondered if maybe he was jealous of her success. She knew Brad's office was an absolute disaster, his organizational skills were next to zero, and he often made bad judgement calls, causing him to waste precious hours of a day.

He seemed intelligent enough, but if that were the case, why couldn't he see how people really viewed him? A nice guy, but a braggart and a bullshitter. She wondered if she should tell him. But how do you tell a friend something like that without insulting them? Impossible. She felt some things were better left unsaid.

"No realtor in this city does what I do," Brad continued. "That's what I told him. No one can do what I do. If you work with me, you're getting 20 years of financial planning expertise. What do you think?" Brad finally asked her.

Debbie hadn't heard him, but thought she could fake it. He often talked about how he would help clients buy a property below market value, refinance it after renovations to pull out all of their down payment, rent it at break even, and move on to buy another one. This wasn't rocket science, and Brad did have a knack for finding properties below market value. He just didn't have to keep repeating it over and over. But now wasn't the time to rain on his parade, as Debbie had other things on her mind. In any event, he was often able to impart valuable financial advice to his clients. And he had a God complex about it.

"Well, you've always been good at that, haven't you?" she said.

"That's what I told him," Brad continued. "And I think he's finally starting to get it."

"You might have to keep telling him," Debbie said.

"What?" He looked at her quizzically, trying and gauge whether she was mocking him.

"You know, until he gets it. Like, completely gets it."

"Oh no, he gets it," Brad said. "He's totally thrilled at what I've done for him, and he's told me so."

Debbie didn't know what he had done for him, but suspected it was the purchase of a house, renovation, and refinance. Wasn't that one of the things Brad always did, with one client or another? It jogged her memory. And she was right. Purchase, renovate, refinance, rent. She even thought she knew the client's name. "Wasn't that Fred?" she asked.

"Yeah, Fred, that's right."

"Oh, you've told me that one before. I remember him. Is he moving on to buy another one, then?"

"He's getting pre-approved for another mortgage as we speak." Brad smiled proudly.

Debbie observed how easily he breached the client confidentiality rules governing realtors.

She wondered what Brad had told his friends about her situation and reminded herself to play it down next time he asked. If there was one thing Debbie had learned, it was never to divulge too much to anyone about your own personal financial situation. First of all, it was none of their business.

Secondly, what they learned they may well use against you.

Thirdly, friends are often jealous of your success and secretly want you to fail.

"How's your year been going?" Brad asked, right on cue.

"Good. Could be better. Could be a lot worse."

Brad smiled. "Look, honey, I know you're one of the top dogs in our office. I study the solds and pendings every morning for two hours. I know which realtors in this city are making money and which ones are starving."

Debbie tried to change the subject. "Do you still get up at four-thirty in the morning and look at pendings and solds?" She was starting to feel a little frustrated by Brad's self-righteous attitude. "What a useless thing to do with your time. Where do you think that info is going to get you? You should be prospecting for clients, reading real estate articles, organizing your office, anything but studying pendings and solds."

Debbie knew Brad was useless at managing his money. And, despite his claims of this deal and that deal, he was always forgetting to pay bills. He was often hounded by bill collectors over minor unpaid bills. Brad had proudly explained once, "I'm too busy and I don't have time to open mail."

"I wanna know who's making money and who isn't so I can only deal with the top realtors," Brad replied, and then rolled his eyes up inside of his head, searching it to see if he had given the right response.

"Well, I believe your time would be better spent doing more productive things. First of all, if you're up at four-thirty in the morning, that should tell you something. It's still dark out, and nobody wants to talk to you at that time. Go back to bed."

Luckily, her phone rang and she didn't have to go through this exercise in futility any longer. She gave Brad a quick hug, and told him she had to leave to deal with an offer.

"Good luck with it," he said to her, gawking at the back of her shapely legs and buttocks as she left. "We should do lunch sometime."

Debbie smiled and left. Like clockwork, Don rolled up in the Lexus. She hopped in, wondering what made her have these bi-weekly coffee breaks with Brad. If your friends are a reflection of you, "then what the fuck does that make me?" she said aloud, and then realized she was on the phone with a realtor.

"Sorry," she said into the phone. "Go ahead and send it through. I'll be at my home office shortly."

Chapter Thirty-Two

Ella tossed and turned on the hard mattress. Or at least she thought she was tossing and turning. She was supposed to be in a coma. At one point in the night, she heard doors slamming upstairs, and a man sobbing and yelling. She couldn't make out all of what he was saying, but thought she heard him say "I didn't mean to do it," at one point, punctuated by more sobs and loud door slamming. She thought of investigating the disturbance, but changed her mind. This wasn't her house, after all. She had no idea whose house it might be, but she thought the voice sounded an awful lot like Earl's.

Through the small bedroom window, she stared at the moon, glowing full and white in the distance. The wind whistled outside and she gripped the small blanket, pulling it up to her chin for warmth. She had left her bedroom door open a crack and felt heat from the fire emanating into the bedroom, warming her. She curled into a fetal position for more warmth and stared at the bright moon. She heard voices coming from outside. She tried to decipher the words. Then she heard it. "... Hereby sentenced to death." And the room went quiet again.

Her curiosity got the better of her. She jumped out of bed and approached the window. She squinted to see in the moonlit night. She noticed a number of tombstones beyond the fenced perimeter. Beyond that, she saw what looked like a gallows, a man standing on the top with a noose around his neck, and a crowd gathered around. The images were black and Ella could not make out any faces.

She felt a tingling on her foot and screamed. A small mouse scattered, finding refuge in a nearby hole in the baseboard.

She trembled with fear.

She wanted to return to bed, but calmed herself, pressing her face to the window. Then she saw a hooded figure pull a lever and the doomed man dropped. The rope around his neck stopped his rapid descent, jerking him upward. Ella swore she heard him moan loudly.

The door slammed upstairs and the loud sobbing voice echoed through the house.

Ella watched the man dangling and twisting in the wind. The crowd of onlookers slowly dispersed. It was all she could take for one night. She ran for the comfort of her bed, jumped in, and pulled the thin blanket up over her head. She panted underneath the covers, still shaking with fear. Her heartbeat slowly returned to normal as the strange sounds subsided.

The next morning she sat at the fireplace, warming herself. Earl greeted her with a cup of tea. He appeared out of sorts, far from the composed man he had been the previous night. His hair was disheveled and his eyes were bloodshot, as if he had been crying.

At this moment Ella was more preoccupied with what was going on around her than her own plight.

"What happened last night?" she asked, sipping her tea.

Earl stared at the fire, silent.

She heard a creaking sound upstairs. Earl's head jerked, his eyes widening with fear. Ella instinctively moved closer to the fire as the intensity of the wind outside increased. The sky was becoming darker. Snow was whipping against the glass.

The creaking stopped.

"You are in the town that I grew up in, Burlington, Prince Edward Island," Earl said. "When I was 20, my girlfriend at the time was Mona. Well," Earl paused, cocking his ear to the second floor. Satisfied he heard nothing, he continued. "Mona became pregnant with my child. She was only seventeen, and she came from a family of much lesser bloodlines than my own. One night I got into the bottle, some powerful moonshine that was going around back then. You have to remember this took place in 1888, around the time of prohibition."

"Okay."

"The poison got the better of me, you see. I knew my parents would be devastated if they found out I got Mona pregnant, they would never let me marry her, and I would be cast out from the family. So I picked up my father's handgun, went over to her house, shot and killed her and dumped her body in the river over there." Earl buried his face in his hands momentarily before continuing. "They hung me for it," he said. "I was the last man to be publicly executed in PEI."

He looked into the fire. "Now I spend my days in this house, trying to make peace with the ghost of Mona. I feel awful about it, and if I could turn back time, I would. I just try to keep the people I meet straight, you know, with good values. I try and instill them with what I could never get. Forget about society's expectations, your parent's expectations, and follow your heart. I made one mistake, a huge mistake, and murdered the only woman I ever truly loved. And her unborn child. My unborn child. Don't you make that same mistake."

"I don't want to do that," Ella said. "It's never entered my mind."

The stairs creaked again and Earl disappeared.

Ella crinkled her brow, trying to remember the events of last night. Earl upstairs slamming doors, sobbing. He must have been talking to Mona. The gallows, the hanging, that was him. He must have to relive that over and over again. Ella shuddered with the thought.

Chapter Thirty-Three

Muskeg had Pickles cornered in the living room. He arched his back and barked. Susan was in her bedroom studying, Garnet on the couch crouched over his notebook, composing music.

Helen and Bob were in the kitchen, drunk again and arguing.

Pickles eyed the barking dog nervously.

"Shut the fuck up, will ya?" Bob yelled.

Muskeg inched closer and that was all it took.

Pickles leaped on the dog's back, digging his claws in. Muskeg yelped in pain and jumped around, trying to dislodge Pickles.

The dog bumped into an end table, sending a lamp crashing to the floor. The light bulb broke with a pop.

Garnet watched the twirling white and black mass in front of him and almost laughed. But he knew Bob, and particularly Helen, would be pissed.

"Pickles, get off him," Garnet said.

The swirling motion in front of him only sped up. It seemed Pickles had no intention of letting go.

"What in the fuck is going on in there?" Bob called from the kitchen. Helen staggered in the room with a mop, swinging it at Pickles trying to dislodge him. The carnage moved into the kitchen. Helen, Bob, and Garnet followed.

Susan cracked open her bedroom door and peeked out. She thought better of making a guest appearance and closed the door.

"Can't you control your fuckin' animal?" Bob screamed at Garnet. "Get yer fuckin' cat off my fuckin' dog for fucksakes."

Helen swung the mop. One of her swings upset a couple of full, open bottles on the kitchen table. They crashed to the floor and shattered.

She charged the animals again, bringing her next swing down with much more authority.

The animals had slowed somewhat, and it seemed certain this swing would connect with Pickles and dislodge him.

It was almost as if he knew. He looked up at the swinging mop, and before it could make contact with him, he leaped from Muskeg's back and raced into Susan's bedroom, just as she had opened the door for another peak at the action.

The mop came down hard, squarely on Muskeg's back, and he yelped again in pain. He ran into the living room and hid underneath the couch.

"I want you and yer animal the fuck outta' here by the end of the week," Bob screamed. "Look what yer doin' to our peaceful life here."

"Okay, okay," Garnet said, retreating into the bedroom.

Chapter Thirty-Four

"Emptiness, that's all I feel is emptiness." Debbie's words startled even herself as she didn't realize she had spoken them aloud. She was sitting at her desk, finishing up some paperwork before turning in for the evening, and her mind had started to drift.

She thought about her business accomplishments, her long list of failed relationships, her current inner circle of friends, her future goals, her material possessions, the nightmares she had been having of late, her failing energy level. She was disappointed that none of those memories created even the semblance of a smile. Quite the opposite.

They made her depressed.

She tried to think of something that gave her pleasure and couldn't. Then Ella popped into her mind. And she did smile this time at the thought of being able to help someone less fortunate than herself. She smiled at the way Ella's crooked smile always seemed to cheer her up, although the woman had very little reason to smile.

She smiled at Ella's inability to believe that she would probably never rise past anything other than a menial, low paying job. In her case, ignorance really was bliss, Debbie thought as she decided a trip to the hospital was in order.

First, she called Garnet. A recording told her the number was no longer in service.

She knew Ella didn't have a phone at the hospital. And something about Ella had been nagging at the back of her mind all day. She'd had a nightmare about Ella the night before and had woken soaked in sweat, petrified, shivering cold.

In her nightmare, she was walking through a forest when she came upon a dilapidated old house by a graveyard. In the graveyard, there was a gallows set up, and she stopped to witness a public execution. As she watched the man die at the end of a rope, she had heard a bloodcurdling scream coming from the house.

She was sure she saw Ella's silhouette peering through a small main-floor window. As the spectators slowly dispersed from the execution, Debbie tried to run to the house in the hope of rescuing her friend.

But her legs wouldn't move.

She tried to call Ella, but no words came.

She woke up panting, and realized it had been a nightmare. She looked at the clock. Three thirty-three am. She got up to go to the bathroom and realized she was so sweat-soaked she had to change her pajamas.

When she returned to bed, the image of the public execution and of Ella screaming stayed with her. Unable to sleep, she lay awake, tossing until 6:00 am, when she finally got up for work.

An hour and twenty minutes later, she sat next to Ella, looking at her in a comatose state, watching her eyes flutter eerily. This sent chills up Debbie's spine. She had bumped into Dr. Carsdale on the way in and he mentioned she had just missed Garnet and Susan, who had spent a couple of hours at Ella's bedside earlier. No, he didn't know if Garnet had a new phone number. Yes, he did know Garnet had been evicted from his last townhouse and was now staying with an uncle.

Ella's heart rate fluttered erratically, and Debbie placed her hand on the woman's arm.

"You're going to be okay, sweetie. I just know it." She knew nothing of the sort, but it made her feel better to say something, anything to Ella.

Chapter Thirty-Five

Ella felt her heart rate increase as she stood looking at the gravestone of Mona Milner. She was bundled up in a thick black woolen shawl, compliments of her host, Earl Milton. She had walked through three-foot snowdrifts and blowing snow to find the marker, leaving deep footprints. The wind howled around her and she felt its cold bite reddening her cheeks.

She wanted to at least honour Mona. After all, it looked as if she would be hanging around for a while, and Ella certainly didn't want to piss this woman off. It was her property, after all. Best to respect the dead.

She knelt down beside the grave and prayed.

The sky darkened, the wind intensified, and a howling sound started off in the distance; faint at first, but then increasing in volume as her prayer neared its end.

"Rest in peace, may God be with you," Ella said, searching for the origin of the howling. The sound stopped, and she heard the faint cry of an infant coming from the nearby woods. The whipping snow and dim light of dusk was making visibility difficult.

Ella turned and trudged through the snow toward the house. She was careful to keep to her original footprints to avoid getting snow inside her boots. On the way out, some snow had slid down inside her boots, and now her toes were becoming numb. She could barely hear the baby's cry now as she approached the porch. The whistling wind carried most of it into the forest.

By the time she reached the door to the house, her toes and face were numb. She looked forward to sitting by the raging fire with a hot cup of tea. She stumbled in, kicked off her boots to drain the water, ice and snow, and went into the living room. She put her boots close to the fire, removed her socks, and enjoyed the warmth of the flames as they infused life back into her cold extremities.

She heard a door creak upstairs and froze. She had yet to become accustomed to the eerie sounds of this strange house.

Earl entered the room with a hot cup of tea and handed it to her. He sat down beside her. Today he looked particularly haggard. The upper door creaked again and Earl jerked his head in the direction of the noise; it seemed to scare him as much as it did Ella. The noise disappeared as quickly as it had come.

She nervously sipped the tea. Earl asked, "How was your little walk in the garden?"

"Uhh, cold." Ella didn't know what else to say. "It's, a, it's a graveyard out there."

There was a long silence, then Earl finally said. "It's where most of my family is buried."

Ella hesitated before saying, "I visited Mona's tombstone, said a little prayer for her."

The upstairs door creaked again and Earl's head jerked. The noise stopped and he refocused his weary gaze on Ella. "That's good," he said. "She could use a few prayers."

They sat in silence, staring at the fire.

Finally, Earl said, "I was hoping you could help me free Mona and my child from this misery."

"How can I do that?"

"You see, like you and I right now, she's trapped in this midway point between heaven and hell, in this house. Like a kind of purgatory. And so is my child. They don't deserve to be here. They both need to move on. It infuriates her to no end. You see, it's all my fault. I brought them here, to try and make peace after killing her, but I've realized over the years it's not going to happen. Her soul exists in a constant state of turmoil, unable to find a peaceful resting place. I want you to help them find a resting place."

"How?" Ella began to put her dry socks on.

"Take them with you. That is what you have to do to leave."

She stopped at the words, one sock dangling from her foot, halfway on. "But I'm not ready to go to heaven right now, so how can I take them with me?"

"I'm not sure," Earl said. "But you have a very positive attitude, maybe you can figure something out. Most of the other lost souls in this place, like myself, are eternally doomed to this damnation, so they're basically useless to her. Not so in your case. You have a chance of returning from your coma, returning to your family. I love Mona, but I can't get her into a frame of mind where she can move on. Maybe she needs to forgive me, but right now I don't think she can do that."

The upstairs door creaked and, as if punctuating Earl's words, slammed shut. A black, hooded apparition raced across the living room, causing a cold chill. The apparition let out a long, moaning scream as it passed. The flames flickered. Ella inched closer to the fireplace, shivering with cold again.

"This place is beginning to scare me," she said. "All I want is to go back home, be with my family."

"Well, I didn't put you here."

"Help me leave, please."

"I'll help you if you help me."

"How will you help me?"

"You'll find out. Go up and see Mona, please."

"No. I'm going to bed." Ella stood up, her knees quivering, and she almost lost her balance. She put her hand on the nearby chair for support, ran to her bedroom, and closed the door.

Now, bundled up in the covers, she wondered if she had been too brash in dismissing Earl. After all, she wanted out of here and wanted out in a hurry.

Chapter Thirty-Six

"I want that right shoe a lot shinier. What's wrong with you, anyway?" the customer asked Garnet. Bud, who was cutting a client's hair, glanced over briefly, then went about his business.

Garnet felt his cheeks redden. He had worked the polishing cloth over each shoe equally, or so he thought. But now, looking down at the two shoes, it appeared the right shoe was smudgy, the left shiny.

"Sorry, sir," he said. "Let me get that." He picked up the polishing cloth again and went to work, this time noticing he wasn't able to put the same amount of force on it with his right hand.

Garnet cursed silently to himself. He re-worked the shining cloth so he could hold it with his right hand and work it back and forth with his left, an effort to compensate for his disability. *I sure can't lose this job*, he thought, noticing his new technique was working.

He stopped, inspected his results. Satisfied, looked up at the customer. "Is that better, sir?"

"It's much better," the man said. He stood, paid, and left. Another customer sat down in the chair and Garnet busied himself with the next pair of shoes. He noticed his new technique worked much better, and he smiled to himself as he went to work.

Bud noticed his delight and winked at him.

An hour later, he limped down the street, his gimped right hand held in an awkward position, looking for a place to call home. He knew he couldn't afford much, which was why he was walking in a seedy, rooming house section of the city. Bud, sensing his desperation, had advanced him five hundred dollars; a real bonus, since that was the only money Garnet had.

He hoped it was enough to find an apartment. He knew he had to get out of Bob's house by tomorrow, and he wondered about the impact these kinds of transitions were having on his daughter.

He passed a run-down building with a sign that read, "Room for Rent. Inquire Within."

He stopped in front of the building, examining it. An old brick four-storey walk-up, with no balconies and no parking. Probably anyone who lived here couldn't afford to own a car anyway. He walked up the steps to the front door. Opening the large wood-framed door, he noticed the pungent odour of cigarette smoke mixed with alcohol.

Garnet wasn't a smoker. And he certainly wasn't much of a drinker, but he needed a place. He was running out of time. There was a series of buzzers inside the door. He pressed the one that read "Mgm't" in faded black lettering.

Nothing happened. A fat man reeking of cheap liquor bumped into him on the way out, muttering "Watch where yer fuckin' goin."

Garnet ignored him, checked his watch, and buzzed again. He had a half hour to get to his employment preparedness course. He was considering quitting the course now that he was gainfully employed.

A skinny, unshaven man with bloodshot eyes and tobacco breath came to the door. "Kin I do ya fer?" he asked Garnet.

"I'm looking for an apartment for my daughter and myself."

"This way," the man said, leading Garnet up the stairs. "It sure ain't much, and it ain't that big fer two people, but come have a look."

They passed an attractive brunette in the stairwell. She was brushing her flowing black hair as she walked and wore a sexy black dress that showed plenty of leg and plenty of cleavage. Her face was caked with make-up.

The caretaker ignored her, but she smiled and winked at Garnet.

Another flight of stairs and they were in the apartment. Furnished sparsely, it was painted grey, with old hardwood floors throughout. One room served as the living room, bedroom and kitchen, and there was a large bathroom with an old claw foot tub. Large, dirt-stained windows overlooked a busy street, and the traffic noise below, although audible enough, wasn't unbearable.

"It's four hundred a month. We don't want lotsa' noise, drugs, partying, that sort of thing around here."

"Do you have an application?"

"No applications. You wan' it, gimme $300 damage deposit and $400 rent an' you can move in tomorrow. I'll have Alice clean it up a bit ."

"I want it, but I only have $400. Can I give you the damage deposit in two weeks?"

"That'd be fine," the man said, shaking Garnet's hand. "I'm Clyde, by the way."

Twenty minutes later, Garnet sat on the bus, heading for his course. He checked his watch. He was going to make it on time. He looked at his rent receipt, his new keys, and the only $100 he had to his name. He smiled. The beginning of a new life.

During lunch, Garnet and Chaddie exchanged stories of success and failure.

"Every company I have ever worked for in the last six years has gone bankrupt," Chaddie said. He listed four companies that had gone under and groaned. "So you see why I don't have a lot of confidence. Then my sister ups and dies a few years back, and my Mom gets hit by a truck, becomes permanently disabled, now I'm stuck at home looking after her. No privacy, man. No social life. Sucks, I'll tell ya. Sometimes hard to keep a positive attitude."

"Don't feel bad," Garnet said. "I just got evicted from my townhouse, had to move in with my drunk uncle, he kicks us out and my wife has slipped into a coma. And she has to come out of the coma because she has a brain tumour that must be operated on. Soon!"

Chaddie, who usually had a lot to say, just stared at Garnet.

"Sorry, bud, thought if you heard how bad my situation was, maybe you'd feel better about your own."

Chaddie frowned as he bit into his apple.

"I've got some good news, though."

"Yeah, what's that?"

"I found a new apartment, temporary, just till we can get on our feet, and I found a job."

Chaddie smiled as Garnet explained about the job and the apartment. He left out the part about being bumped by the drunkard and passing a hooker in the stairwell.

Chapter Thirty-Seven

Ella awoke abruptly to the sound of a door slamming, and screaming.

"Please forgive me," a voice cried from the upper floor.

Ella listened, stiff with fear. She hopped out of bed, threw on a shawl, and lit a candle. She slowly made her way to her bedroom door. It creaked, swinging open all the way. She held up the candle. It faintly illuminated the hallway to the stairwell. She stood and listened.

Not a sound.

She took one step. The floorboards creaked. She felt her heart rate increase as she started walking up the stairs. As she neared the landing on the second floor, a bedroom door flew open and a beautiful blonde woman in a transparent negligee stepped out. She wiped her eyes and looked at Ella, disapproval etched in her features. Then she ran, or rather flew, into a room at the far end of the long hallway.

Ella looked into the open door and saw Earl sitting on the bed, his head slumped over, both hands covering his face.

She sat beside Earl, and put her arm around his shoulder. "Tell me what you want me to do, Earl. Do you want me to go see Mona?"

He looked up at her, eyes watery and bloodshot. "Please see what you can do. I beg you."

Ella leaned over, kissing him gently on the cheek.

"I'll see what I can do." She left the room and walked toward the room she had seen Mona enter. The door was shut, so she politely knocked.

"Mona, are you in there?"

She could hear sobs on the other side of the door. She knocked again. "Mona, may I come in and talk to you?"

She heard a faint voice from the other side of the door. "What do you want?"

"I just want to talk."

The house was quiet except for the sound of the blowing wind outside.

"What can you possibly say that will change anything?"

Ella had no idea, but she knew somehow their fates were inextricably linked.

She noticed Earl was retreating downstairs.

"Come in."

Ella opened the door and walked in. Mona sat at a make-up table before a mirror, combing her long, flowing blonde hair. The room was immaculate, unlike any of the others Ella had been in. An open window beside the bed blew transparent curtains in different directions.

No reflection of her could be seen in the mirror, although Ella did notice her own reflection as she spoke.

"Do you mind if I close this window?"

"Suit yourself."

Ella closed the shutters. "Can I sit on your bed to talk to you?" she asked, squeezing her shawl tightly over her body, trying to take the chill off.

"Of course."

Trying to settle her nerves, Ella finally asked, "Do you like this place where you're at?"

"What's there to like?"

"Would you like to leave?"

"How do you propose I do that?"

"I think what's holding you back is your unwillingness to forgive Earl."

Mona's features grew dark. "Why should I forgive that old fool?"

"Maybe it's the key to you moving on from this dark place."

Mona turned around in her chair, looking at Ella squarely. "Do you know what he did to me? Did he tell you he shot me, threw my body in the river? Did he tell you I was pregnant at the time? Would you forgive someone like that?"

"I know those things," Ella said. "And, yes, I would forgive, if it would free my soul from purgatory."

Mona seemed to be contemplating it when suddenly the window shutters flew open with such force they crashed into the bedroom wall, shattering glass in all directions.

Mona jerked around, staring at the window.

Ella felt the thump of her heart. She tried to will the fear away, but it crept up her body, stiffening the tiny hairs on the small of her back.

"You don't know what kind of evil forces you're up against, lady," Mona said. "You might never get out of here yourself."

Then she vanished.

A mist entered the room and morphed into the shape of a black, monster-like demon. Red eyes penetrated Ella. The demon raised a hand, pointed a finger in her direction, and made a low growling sound that slowly grew louder.

Ella tried to leave.

Too late.

The raging fury of the beast was upon her. He thrust her into the air and flung her into the door. She crashed partway through the lower panel, wood splintering with a crunch.

She wondered in that instant if she was meant to die here and go straight to hell like everybody else. She willed herself to her feet.

Too late again.

The demon threw her into the wall. She hit it with a thud, and the plaster cracked, leaving a near-perfect impression of her head. She wilted down the side of the wall, looking up at the indentation, wondering if she was dreaming. It seemed awfully similar to the accident she had before her coma.

"No," she screamed.

A loud banging at the door. Earl's voice. "Ella, Ella, open the door. Are you okay?"

"Help!"

Earl passed through the splintered door, carrying a large axe, and began swinging it at the demon. The beast ducked a couple of swings before flying up in the air, then out through the open window.

"Don't be afraid of him," Earl said a few minutes after he had helped Ella walk down the stairs and into the kitchen. "He can't hurt you if you don't want him to."

Sitting at the kitchen table, Ella wasn't so sure. Her head hurt.

"He preys on weakness. If you show it, you're in trouble. He wants me, Mona, and the child. And, I guess since you're here, he'll probably include you in the mix."

"He's not going to include me in any mix," Ella said resolvedly. "Not if I can help it."

"I think he'll get me, and I'll go to hell. But I just want to save Mona and the child. They don't deserve this. Then I'll gladly go with him, end my miserable existence here."

"What else do you want me to do?"

"The child. Go to him."

"Where is he?"

"In the woods. Bring him in the house, look after him. Mona will be so glad to see him."

Ella was still rattled from her encounter with the demon. "I'll look for him in the morning. I'm going to finish my tea, then try and get some rest."

Lying in her bed, Ella tried to make sense of her situation. It was all so strange. But she was going to try to make things right between Mona and Earl.

As she drifted off, she heard the soft wail of a baby crying. It was off in the distance, but the sound permeated her room hauntingly. She shifted to her side, burying one ear in the pillow and cupping her hand over the other ear. She didn't want to hear it. Not now, anyway. And she certainly didn't want to go out in the cold, in the dead of night, looking for the child.

"He's a spirit," she said to herself, cupping her hand tighter over her ear. "If he survived this long, he'll survive another night out there."

Besides, what was her game plan if she encountered the demon again? Will him to go away? She wasn't sure that would work. She slipped into a deep sleep.

The following morning she got up and went outside. In this state of flux, she didn't seem to require any food or nourishment, other than the tea. The sun shone brightly and the sky was clear blue, although it was still crisp with cold. She stepped off the porch, squinting in the sun, unaccustomed to its glare. Since she had been here, and she had completely lost track of the days. It always seemed eerily dark.

She tiptoed around the cemetery, again taking care to follow most of her old tracks—at least what was left of them. The jagged limb of the old apple tree had snapped off in the previous night's storm, and she took care to step over it. About an acre and a half around the house had been cleared many years ago, by the looks of it. Beyond the cemetery, there was a big, grey wooden barn leaning precariously to one side, as if it might fall over at any time. Beyond that, the tree line, and a path that led through it. The one she had taken to get here, she was almost sure.

Not sure where she was going, she decided to follow the path.

After walking about fifty feet under cracking branches, she came upon a clearing in the bush. She spotted animal tracks. *Bear tracks, maybe? No ... they looked more like the tracks of wolves.*

She heard a single howl that built into a loud crescendo of accompanying howls. A pack of wolves. She wanted to turn around, but something willed her forward. It seemed the sound was coming from just beyond the little clearing.

Gathering courage, she walked toward the sound. Twigs snapped under her feet. She heard a snarl.

Then she saw them: a pack of black wolves gathered around their prey, feeding. She advanced and then stopped, frozen to the spot.

Two black wolves looked up from their feeding, their snouts and lower jaws dripping red. One snarled at her, showing its bloody fangs, drops of blood staining the white snow below it. Its yellow eyes regarded her cautiously.

She was about to turn and run when she heard a rustling sound in the distance. The wolves stopped, turned momentarily toward the sound, then scattered quickly into the bush. A few of them punctuated their exit with short howling bursts.

Ella listened, waiting.

Nothing.

Curious, she walked over to the spot where the wolves had been feeding. She wanted to know if they had eaten the little child, although she wasn't entirely sure how that could be possible.

Thoroughly confused, she reached the killing ground. Blood and entrails covered the area, and it was hard to make out what the corpse was. Large chunks were missing from the body. She bent closer, trying to get a better look.

Then she saw it. The foot was human, and the rest of the mangled torso was that of a man. But it had a pig's head. Mangled and bloody, but definitely a pig.

Although frightened, she couldn't take her eyes off it.

The howling of the wolves drew nearer. They wanted to return to their kill, finish their lunch.

She turned and ran toward the house.

By the time she stopped, she realized she was beside the old barn. She took deep breaths and listened, sure now that the wolves would gain on her in an instant, attack en masse, and tear her apart limb by limb.

Between breaths, she listened.

She heard nothing but the snarling and chomping of wolves off in the distance, devouring what was left of pig beast.

What kind of creatures exist in this forest?

Her heart rate slowed and she surveyed her surroundings.

What she saw made her gasp. Bloody footprints in the snow led into the old barn.

She followed them, pulling the old door. It creaked loudly as it swung open. The smell of death assaulted her nostrils. A rotting corpse, to be sure. It was a moment before her eyes adjusted to the dimly lit interior. The smell was so rancid she almost puked. She coughed and brought her hand to her nose. She knew she wouldn't be able to last long here.

The interior was old boards, an uneven wooden floor, some hay, and three horse stalls.

As her eyes adjusted to the light, she noticed the bloody footprints leading into one of the stalls.

The stench was overpowering. She flung open the door, stepped outside, and took a deep breath of fresh air. Then she held her breath and re-entered.

She quickly followed the footprints to the last stall in the barn. As she passed the second stall, she noticed what was likely the source of the stench. It was a dead racoon, curled up in the fetal position.

Must've frozen to death, she thought.

She looked in at the last stall and saw some bales of hay had been fashioned into a bed of sorts, as if for a small animal.

Or a baby.

She looked in the makeshift crib. It was red and crusty on the outside. The inside was strewn with dry hay, and appeared to have none of the blood-red stains.

Then she noticed it. A small silver baby rattle.

She picked it up and ran out of the barn, inhaling deeply the moment she cleared the doorway.

The baby. He's in here. At least, sometimes he is. She was sure. Vowing to return at dusk, she walked back to the old house.

It was eerily quiet and dark inside, despite the bright sunlight outside. The fire barely burned, but some hot embers remained and she held her hands over them briefly before deciding to explore the rest of the house. She walked down the long hallway to the end, planning on working her way back to her room. There were four other rooms to explore before she got there. She opened the door to the first.

It was a small bedroom full of cobwebs and, but for a single bed and a small nightstand with a pipe and some tobacco, barren of furnishings.

She was about to close the door when she noticed a picture on the night table. She picked it up, and recognized the images of Earl and Mona, much younger and locked in an embrace, both smiling happily at the photographer.

She put it down and left, not wanting to snoop around what little personal belongings Earl possessed.

The second room was a master bedroom with an adjoining ensuite bath. It was huge and furnished richly with Victorian-style furniture, including plush red velvet window coverings.

As she entered, she felt a cold chill. She looked around and saw a white, misty shape, barely visible in the bathroom. It was Mona. She possibly had two bedrooms.

"Is this what you do? Snoop in other people's houses, go through other people's belongings?" she asked, sitting on the bed.

"I'm sorry," Ella said. "I'll leave now."

"What is that you have?"

Ella looked at her hand, realizing she was still carrying the baby rattle. "Oh, uh, I found this in the barn."

"Put it in the baby's room, will you?"

"Yes, of course."

She turned to leave, then glanced back. Mona was gone.

The next room she entered contained a crib. Ella walked in, put the rattle in the crib, and left.

She decided to forego opening the last door.

Back in the living room, she threw a log in the burning embers and took her seat by the fire. She wondered when it would be best to return to the barn.

"Earl," she said, almost without realizing it.

No response.

"Mona," she called, eager for some company.

Silence.

She hadn't realized how tired she was until she found her eyes beginning to close. It wasn't long before she drifted off.

Chapter Thirty-Eight

Garnet stared at his computer keyboard. The traffic hummed outside, the volume becoming lower as the tail end of rush hour commuters made their way home.

Susan sat by the window, listening to her iPod. Garnet could hear the faint echoes of rap over the din of traffic, but it didn't bother him.

Pickles stretched on Susan's crossed legs. Even he seemed relieved at the reprieve from the yappy poodle Muskeg. However, he did have one eye open, and it glanced furtively around the room, finally fixing on Garnet.

They had moved into the apartment yesterday, thanks to Chaddie's assistance.

When they had arrived at Bob's to pick up their things, Bob and Helen were at their usual best—sufficiently drunk.

Chaddie, however, also reeked of cigarettes and alcohol, so Garnet wasn't sure how this was going to go over. He remembered Chaddie telling him previously he had ten years of boxing and martial arts training. Although Chaddie might be prone to embellishing certain stories, Garnet certainly didn't take him for a bullshitter.

And as soon as Uncle Bob started ranting, Chaddie cut him off. "If I were you, I would keep your fuckin' mouth shut while we move this shit out," he had said. "What kind of uncle kicks his nephew out on the street three days after he moves in, anyway?"

Bob was about to retort, but Chaddie stepped toward him, clenching his fists.

Garnet could tell his friend must have been in more than a few street brawls. Chaddie certainly hadn't mentioned any that he had lost, but he had a bridge replacing five upper teeth. Sometimes when he talked, he would rotate the mouthpiece in and out of its position, exposing bare gums.

As they drove away in the black pick-up truck, loaded up with the last of Garnet's possessions, Garnet looked back. Bob had a rake in one hand and was flipping them off with the other; Helen had a beer in one hand, and was waving the other, maybe trying to absolve herself; and, of course, Muskeg was barking incessantly.

He looked at his computer and sighed.

"You okay, Dad?" Susan asked, cocking one of the headphones above one ear so she could hear his response.

"Fine, honey." Garnet looked at the piece he was composing, saved it, and turned the computer off. He couldn't concentrate on his music. Ella had been in a coma for some time, and he was worried.

"I think we should go," he said to his daughter.

On cue, Pickles jumped from Susan's lap and waited at the door.

Susan removed her headphones and set the iPod down on a table. "Oh no, Pickles, you can't come. Look, Dad, he wants to come with us."

"Meeeeeooow?"

"No, Pickles, stay here."

"Let's go, Susan."

"Okay. I'm just going to call Hank."

Garnet walked into the bathroom to give his daughter some privacy. Since her job at McDonald's, she had made some money for a minute card for her pay-as-you-go phone. It was the only working phone the Dewitt family had.

My daughter's growing up fast, Garnet thought as he splashed water on his face and dried himself with a towel. Lately, he noticed she had been spending more time with Hank, and he wondered when the day would come when he would hardly ever see her.

He reckoned sadly that day wasn't too far away. He knew full well he had not been able to provide for her like he wanted.

He heard her say goodbye as he came out of the bathroom.

"Can I see Hank tonight, after the hospital?"

He forced a smile. "Sure, honey, whatever you like."

Chapter Thirty-Nine

"I'm just checking in to see how you are."

"Okay," Debbie said, a little surprised.

"The last time we talked, you seemed, I don't know, a little out of sorts. Are you okay?" Brad asked.

Debbie was on her way to a ReMax awards ceremony when he called. It rattled her, as Brad usually called for shop talk, most of which Debbie was completely uninterested in.

Now she felt bad for thinking so badly of him and being so critical.

Debbie was usually pretty good at putting her game face on and not showing her emotions. But, if she had to be completely honest, her image of herself as a rock had started to crumble in a few spots.

But she didn't want to admit to that right now. At least, not on the phone, on the way to an awards ceremony, with Don listening.

"Look, Brad, honey, I feel great, honest I do. I just must've had an off day when we met for coffee. Everyone's entitled, right?"

"Sure. Listen, did I catch you at a bad time?"

"I'm on my way to the office awards banquet. Aren't you coming?"

"No offense, but I don't play well with a bunch of realtors."

"Okay. Listen, thanks for the call. We'll catch up soon." She clicked off the phone as her vehicle pulled into the parking lot of the Glenmore Inn.

Debbie had a lump in her throat as her driver sped away. She felt ashamed for thinking that Brad was too self-centred and narcissistic to give a shit about her.

He obviously did.

She walked into the building and found her seat at a large table of realtors at the banquet. She sipped a glass of white wine. The room hummed with chatter and laughter as they waited for the awards ceremony to begin.

"For sure you will be in the top ten, if not number one, this year," her co-worker Peggy said.

Debbie smiled, trying to lift the heaviness that had settled over her. Right now, being number one, or number ten for that matter, didn't really mean much to her.

Kind of surprising, given the fact that in previous years she would not only follow the top realtors monthly, but strive to outdo them prior to the awards ceremonies so she could keep her top spot.

"Don't you think so?" Peggy asked, sipping her wine.

"I worked hard, so I hope so," Debbie said perfunctorily. She watched as Peggy tilted the entire contents of her wine glass into her mouth.

Peggy must be on her fourth or fifth glass of wine. She was becoming giddier, and her words had become slightly slurred.

Usually, the banter with Peggy was light and comical, but Debbie felt herself growing tired of her friend. An attractive woman in her own right, Peggy always dressed to a tee, was the consummate materialist, and generally factored just inside the top ten salespeople in the office. If she did miss the top ten, it usually wasn't by much.

"Look at Paul," she said now, giggling. "Is that a toupee? That looks awful, why not just shave your head and get it over with. Didn't he used to have a comb-over ?"

Debbie nodded and smiled. The toupee did look ridiculous.

Ah, what the hell, she thought, motioning to the waiter walking around with the bottle of white wine. He came over and began to fill her glass..

"I'll have the whole bottle, please," Debbie said, plucking it from his hand and filling first Peggy's glass, then her own.

A few of the other realtors stared at her. She didn't usually let her hair down at company parties.

But Debbie didn't give a shit today. She had begun to feel that living through a mirror of other people's expectations amounted to a betrayal of one's own identity.

"Thata' girl," Peggy said, and they clinked glasses.

"You coming home with me tonight, sweetie?" thirty-year veteran realtor Blake asked her with a wink. "There's more of that in my wine cellar."

Debbie had always admired Blake, now in his late sixties and close to retirement. Not only one of the best realtors in the office, he was also one of the finest people she had ever met. Debbie regarded him as one of her few close friends.

"Guess we're having a party tonight," she said, tilting her glass and emptying the contents. She held it out to Peggy. "More, please."

The awards ceremony commenced. The first fifteen minutes involved talk about technological improvements and the rapid expansion of ReMax around the globe and blah, blah, blah.

By the time Debbie's name was called, she was well on her way to becoming pissed—a first for her at any company party.

"Third place in the office for this year goes to one of our most respected realtors, Debbie Dupree."

Loud clapping.

"Please come up, Debbie, and say a few words."

"Speech, speech, speech," the realtors shouted.

Debbie went to stand, caught a bad angle with one of her stilettos, and stumbled. Blake grabbed her arm and steadied her.

A few people clapped and muttered.

"You okay?" Blake whispered.

"I will be. Thanks."

Debbie tried to clear her head as she approached the podium. She was a cheap drunk and was starting to see two podiums. *Make it, make it, make it*, she said to herself and she finally did, with only a slight stumble just before anchoring herself to the podium.

She received a plaque.

"I wanna thank ReMax for being such a great company to work with," Debbie said, smiling. She, paused, cleared her throat, and continued. "In particular, I would like to thank Blake Edwards for saving my ass just then and preventing me from falling flat on my face. Thanks you, Blake."

Uproarious laughter. She waited for it to quiet down, then continued.

"Kidding aside, I think this is a great office. It's an honour to work with so many awesome realtors. I love all the charity work our office does, and I love you guys. Thank you very much."

Noticing she was a little tipsy, the office manager came to her rescue, providing her with an escort back to her chair.

"Thanks, Steve," she said as he helped her sit.

They reached number ten and Peggy Gilmore's name was called. Debbie stood with her friend, taking her by the arm. Blake took the cue and led Peggy up to the podium. She was wasted.

In between speeches, Debbie laughed and flirted with Blake, something she hadn't done in a long time.

Tomorrow she would probably pay dearly for her little indiscretion, but right now she enjoyed the moment. For the time being, at least, the alcohol had helped alleviate the sinking feeling she'd had earlier.

She vowed that tomorrow she would look at her life head on, figure out what was wrong with it, and try to fix it. Maybe it was the alcohol, but that vow made her smile.

"At least now I'm not in denial," she said to no one in particular as she speed-dialed Don to retrieve her.

Arriving at her Lake Bonavista Estates home, she still felt a little tipsy. Her first thought was to go straight to bed, and then she decided maybe another glass of wine was in order. She cracked a bottle of white wine, poured herself a glass, and sat in front of the TV.

"Who can I call?" she asked aloud, losing interest in the images on the screen. She looked at the clock. It was 10:30 pm, a little late for most people.

She picked up the phone anyway and called Brad. He always answered his phone.

"Hello?" He sounded like he had been sleeping.

"Did I wake you up?"

"Who's this?"

"You don't recognize my voice? Known me for how many years now and don't recognize my voice."

"Debbie? Have you been drinking?"

"A little. Guess what, I placed number three in the office this year."

"Congratulations."

"And you know what else? I've decided to turn my life around, not be so preoccupied with money, success, all that shit."

"Good for you."

"I've realized it's all a bunch of shit, really. I mean, how much of that stuff you accumulate can you take with you when you're dead, anyway?"

"None of it, I guess."

"That's right. When I'm dead and gone do you think I will be remembered by how many toys I accumulated or that I'm number three in the office this year?"

"Debbie ..."

"No, I won't. I'll be remembered by how many people I loved and the depth of love I had for them. Period. Do you know that?"

Brad had never heard Debbie talk like this before.

"Yes, I know that," he said.

"Well, starting tomorrow, I am going to begin giving back. And I'm going to change my life. Do you know how empty and lonely my life feels at times, working, working, working, making deals? For what? I'm sick of it and I need to start something different."

"That's good," Brad said.

"Have I ever told you that I love you?"

She'd never said that to him before. In fact, she had said it very few times in her life to anyone.

"No, but it's okay 'cause I know you do."

"Well, I appreciate you calling to check in on me. Do you know how many of my friends actually do that?"

"No."

"Almost none, other than you, Garnet, and Ella. You're actually one of my best friends. And look at those two. Their lives are completely fucked, but they have one thing a lot of other people don't. Their lives might never amount to shit on a materialistic level, but they plod forward, happy, confidently believing in their goals."

"We can learn a lot from people like them," Brad said.

"Like me," Debbie responded. "I need to see Ella tomorrow, and try and track down Garnet and Susan as well."

Chapter Forty

Garnet and Susan sat and stared at Ella. She was very still, and there was no rapid eye movement this time. They had come last night as well, and stayed for two hours, Garnet holding Ella's hand the entire time.

On that visit, Garnet also had an appointment with his psychologist, physiotherapist and neurologist.

According to Carsdale, Garnet was recovering well, and it appeared the operation was a success, although further monitoring was still required. Dr. Carsdale adjusted his anti-seizure medication.

Garnet had to admit it was nice to be seizure-free. But, looking down at his pale wife now, it was the farthest thing from his mind.

It had been two weeks since the coma, and Ella was not showing signs of coming out of it.

Carsdale hadn't sounded optimistic.

Garnet inched his chair closer so he could hold his wife's hand. Susan, beside him, put her hand on her mother's arm.

"Will she be okay, Dad?"

"I think so, honey. She'll come out of it."

Debbie walked into the room, concern on her face. That morning she had woken up with a pounding headache and she'd had some trouble remembering the previous night's events.

She vaguely remembered telling Brad she loved him. *What an idiot*, she thought as she hugged Susan and Garnet.

Looking down at her friend in a coma, those thoughts evaporated. In the two weeks since her coma, Ella had lost a lot of weight, her complexion had become jaundiced, and her lips were pursed. She looked almost afraid.

"Is she going to be okay?" Debbie asked.

"I think so," Garnet said.

"What did Dr. Carsdale say?" Debbie asked, thinking about her nightmare, seeing Ella trapped in that old house.

"He doesn't know. But I'm confident she'll come out of it."

Chapter Forty-One

Ella stirred in her rocking chair. She woke and saw Earl standing over her, his hand on her arm.

"Ooh, must've fallen asleep," she said, rubbing her eyes.

"It's almost time," Earl said, handing her a hot cup of tea and then depositing another log on the blazing fire.

Ella sipped the tea, rubbing the sleep from her eyes with the other hand. "Does he have a name?"

"Who?"

"The baby."

"Mona calls him Charlie."

"Should I go now?"

"Finish your tea."

Ella could see the sun setting. She didn't have a lot of time. "Is he in the barn?"

"I don't know."

She gulped the last few drops of her tea. "I'm leaving. You have a flashlight?"

"Sorry, no."

"A candle?"

"Yes, in the kitchen. Matches in the cupboard."

She went into the kitchen, found the items, and left.

She followed her footsteps past the cemetery to the barn. It was dusk, and the sun inched over the landscape in the distance.

The wolves began to howl.

She saw yellow eyes staring at her from the tree line. There was just enough light to make out the wolves, but she knew in a minute that would be gone.

The moon rose opposite the setting sun. It was full, so at least it would provide her with some light. She heard some twigs snap to the right of the barn, and saw a black silhouette. She hoped it wasn't the demon.

Keep going.

"First Charlie, then Mona, then back home," she said aloud.

She only hoped it would be that easy.

She was about ten feet away from the barn when she saw it.

More bloody footprints leading to the barn. But this time, there was more than one set of tracks.

A black silhouette rose up from the tree line, took on a monstrous shape, then disappeared in the forest again, an echoing snarl trailing its exit.

The wolves howled at the full moon.

Ella approached the barn. She pulled out the candle and matches. She tried to light it, but her hands were shaking too much. The wind blew the match out. She lit another one and got the candle going.

She took a few steps toward the door.

It came crashing open, connected with her head, and she fell in the snow. The candle rolled away, the flame extinguished in an instant.

The pig beast leaped out, snarled fiercely, and advanced toward Ella. Its feet were covered in blood.

It dove at her and she rolled away.

It landed in the snow, inches from her.

She scrambled to her feet and ran.

She could hear the panting right behind her, feel its cold breath on her neck.

She heard more rustling behind her. It was the wolves. They were coming for her.

She heard a squealing sound. She glanced behind her and realized the wolves were after the pig beast. One of them had lunged at its leg, sunk its teeth into the calf, and was trying to pull it to the ground.

It squealed in pain.

Ella had reached the clearing. She saw a large, overturned log and dove over it, ducking down as she did.

She was gasping for air.

Nothing was chasing her now.

But she could hear the squealing growing louder and more desperate.

She peaked over the toppled tree and saw the wolves had slowed their prey considerably. One still had its teeth clenched onto the calf muscle, blood squirting out as the pig beast rotated, trying to jerk free.

But another wolf had secured a vice-like grip with its fangs on the other leg, and the creature was fighting a losing battle.

Soon, another wolf leaped up, clamping its jaws hard down on the pig beast's throat, and brought it to the ground with a loud thump.

It fell on its back, delivering a powerful blow to the wolf's head as it landed. The wolf rolled off its prey, yelping, and went limp.

Knocked out or dead, Ella thought, watching the action.

Another wolf attacked, biting the beast's throat.

And soon another. And another, and before long there were maybe a dozen wolves tearing, snarling, and chomping at it.

It squealed loudly.

Then it fell silent and went limp.

While the wolves ravaged the beast, Ella circled around them, back to the barn, where she hoped another one wasn't waiting for her.

As she walked, she fished in her pocket. *Good, I still have the matches. But the candle ...* she knew it was somewhere in the snow.

She reached the clearing and started feeling around for it in the snow.

"Found it," she said.

She was about to light it when the demon rose from the black mist in the trees, landing a few feet in front of her.

It growled fiercely, focusing its blood red eyes on Ella.

"No, no no," Ella said. "You get out of here. You don't belong here." She waved the lit candle in front of the demon. The flame flickered, almost going out, but sparked to life again as she steadied it.

She didn't know what to do. Should she run?

At that moment Earl appeared on the porch with a sawed-off shotgun. "Get yer ass in the barn," he said, and levelled a blast of lead at the demon. Startled, it turned its head in Earl's direction.

She hurried into the barn, hoping another pig beast wasn't waiting for her. She slammed the door behind her, fumbled for the matches in the dark, and relit the candle.

The shotgun blasted again.

This horror roller coaster ride didn't make any sense to Ella. If she died here, did that mean she died in the hospital?

She suspected the answer to that question was yes.

The shotgun blast sounded again, and an upper window of the barn shattered. Shards of glass rained down inside.

The demon disappeared.

Another question bothered her. If Earl was the ghost of a dead man, what did he fear from this demon?

Was it the possibility of going to hell?

Didn't he know he was likely going to end up there anyway?

Was he waiting for Mona and Charlie to move on to a peaceful place before he joined the damned?

And how could she kill this demon? And if she couldn't, and it killed her, would that mean she would go to hell?

"Ouch," she said, looking at her finger, where the wax from the burning candle had dripped. *Snap out of it.*

It went quiet.

Carrying the candle, she approached the last stall. Then she saw him.

Wrapped in a white blanket, sleeping soundly with his little thumb in his mouth.

She bent down and picked him up.

Charlie opened his eyes, smiled, and closed them again. She brought him out of the barn and into the clearing.

Earl had turned the back porch light on, and he stood on the porch, waving to her. "Bring him here, quickly," he said.

She bent down, snuffed the candle out in the snow, put it in her pocket, cradled Charlie in both hands, and proceeded into the house. Earl held the door open for her as she entered.

"Where's the demon?" she asked, walking past him.

"That's one of Satan's servants," Earl said, still holding the shotgun. "I scared him off, at least for now."

"Where do you want Charlie?"

"I put the crib in Mona's room, end of the hall. Take him in there." Earl looked at the baby, a mixture of sadness and joy etched in his wrinkled face.

Once inside, she placed him in the crib.

"My baby, my baby," Mona screamed behind her, reaching into the crib.

Ella sat on the bed as Mona gently picked her child up, cradling him lovingly. Charlie opened his eyes, smiling at her.

She turned to Ella. "This is the first time I've ever seen my child, you know."

"I do now."

"Where did you find him?"

"In the barn."

"I've never been able to venture outside," Mona murmured. "I'm confined to this prison."

Earl appeared at the doorway. Mona glared at him. "What right do you have here? You lost your parental rights when you killed both of us. Now go."

"I ... I just wanted to see him," Earl said. "I helped her get him for you."

Charlie began to cry.

"Calm down, both of you," Ella interjected. "Just for the moment, can't you put aside your differences for the sake of your child? Look at him, look what you've gone and done. He's crying."

The two stopped arguing.

Charlie cried.

Ella stood up, caressed the baby's cheek, and smiled. "There, there, Charlie, everything is going to be okay."

He stopped crying. Mona set him gently in the crib and he curled up, inserting his thumb in his mouth.

"Why don't you let Charlie sleep? We can carry on this discussion by the fire," Ella said.

Earl left the room.

Mona stood, admiring her baby. Ella approached her and put her arm gently on her shoulder. Mona started crying.

"It's okay, I understand what you're going through. I have a daughter, and if anyone ever did anything to her, I would ... well, I don't know what I would do, but I would be very upset."

"What do you want me to do?" Mona said, wiping away her tears. "How can I forgive a murderer? Would you be able to forgive someone if they killed your daughter? Would you?"

"Yes, I would. And maybe they wouldn't deserve it, but I think to harbour all that hate is unhealthy. Who is going to suffer more for it, you or the killer?"

"In this case, probably both of us," Mona said.

Ella had to admit she had a point. Earl was a wreck. She tried another approach.

"What about this hellhole you're in? What about Charlie? He's been living in the barn, with demons and pig beasts for the last—who knows how long. Don't you want to free your baby as well?"

"Earl can go straight to hell as far as I'm concerned."

"Maybe that's where he'll end up. Maybe that's why this demon is hanging around here. Earl won't go anywhere until he's sure your soul is happy."

"Do you think if I forgive him, Charlie and I can leave this place?"

"That's what Earl says."

"What does he know?"

"Consider this: Do you know I'm as much trapped here as you are? Earl tells me if I help you, all of you, I get my life back. I get to come out of my coma, go back to my family, which I want to do more than anything."

Mona paused. "How do you know any of this will work?"

"I don't, but don't you think it's worth a try?"

Chapter Forty-Two

It was very dark, but the full moon lit up the sky. At least enough to see where she was going.

But I don't know where I'm going, Debbie thought as she walked through the forest.

"Where the hell am I?" she said to herself, zipping up her jacket. She shivered in the cold wind. The yellow eyes in the forest followed her and howled.

They scared her, and she ran in panic.

She saw a small light, and maybe a clearing at the end of the path. The howling of the wolves grew louder as she ran.

A black mist appeared in front of her, obscuring the light. She stopped in her tracks, panting.

The mist cleared, and now she could see it.

A demon. Blood-red glowing eyes, devilish features, tall, brown, muscle bound.

"Join my world," the demon said to her. "Come and be free."

"I'm not coming with you anywhere."

The demon screamed, a howling scream, advancing toward her.

Debbie tried to scream for help, but only exhaled. She tried running, and finally her legs started moving. She ran around the monster, sprinting along the path toward the light.

She could feel its hot breath on her as she ran.

Then she saw it: a house with a porch light on, illuminating the clearing and a lopsided barn.

Since the barn was closer, she ran inside, slamming the door behind her, clutching the handle to prevent the demon from entering.

It thudded against the door just as she slammed it shut.

"Damn you, woman. You'll be with me soon enough, anyway."

The barn was dark, save for a faint bead of light coming from a broken window.

Ferocious growling sounds inside the barn startled her, and then they attacked. Two muscular beasts with oversized pig-heads. Debbie screamed and ran for the door, but she couldn't open it.

They were upon her instantly, tearing at her flesh with their claws and teeth.

"Ella," she screamed. "Help me, someone help me."

But by now large chunks of flesh were missing from her body, and she felt herself weakening with the rapid blood loss. With one swipe if its claw, one of the beasts severed her jugular vein and blood sprayed like projectile vomit.

She fell to the ground.

Her eyes slowly closed and she went limp.

Chapter Forty-Three

She opened her eyes. She was in bed. She looked around, bewildered, believing for a moment that she was actually dead. Her body was drenched in sweat, and her heart pounded rapidly.

Never in her entire lifetime could she remember having a nightmare in which she actually died, and it terrified her. Sure, she'd had falling dreams, as everyone did, where you wake up just before hitting the ground.

But dying?

She shivered at the thought, the horrific images still fresh in her mind.

Her assistant Lisa walked into the room. She had a key to the house and would sometimes come in early. "Are you okay?"

She didn't look okay. She was soaking wet, her blankets and pillows in complete disarray, most of them had fallen to the floor.

"I had a nightmare, Lisa. I'm fine, but thanks for asking."

"No problem," she said. "By the way, you got a call from Brad, and a call from Garnet."

Debbie looked at her clock: 10:33 am. She had slept in. She usually rose by eight in the morning and had already put in an hour's work before her assistant showed. She hopped out of bed.

"Want some tea?" Lisa asked.

"That would be great. Thank you."

Half an hour later, she sat at her desk, sipping tea. She barked out the usual list of duties for Lisa, reminding her of the top priority jobs.

A tiger might be able to change its stripes. But not easily. And certainly not overnight.

Lisa went to work.

Debbie looked at her massive to-do list and all the calls she had to make. It was a long list.

She called Garnet first.

"What's up, my friend?" she asked, trying to clear the horrific images of her nightmare from her mind.

"I'm starting to worry about Ella."

Debbie had to admit she was getting a little worried herself. She knew her nightmares were connected to Ella. "Do you have an update?"

"Dr. Carsdale called me at work today. He said if Ella's still in a coma in another week, we should consider how much longer we're prepared to wait."

Debbie knew what this meant. That Carsdale was planting the seeds in Garnet's mind about when to pull the plug and end Ella's life. "Aren't there signs of brain activity?"

"Apparently the last EEG showed very little."

"What about all the fluttering eye movement?"

"Doesn't seem to be happening much right now, if at all."

"Listen, Garnet, how about I go down and try and talk to Carsdale this afternoon, get something more conclusive, maybe a ray of hope that we can hang on to."

"Okay. I just don't think it's sounding that good at all."

Debbie bit her lip. Garnet was usually much more positive.

"Another thing before you go," he said. "I know you're very busy, but I don't know how long I can last in this apartment. We have drunks and hookers coming and going all the time. And Susan hardly sleeps here anymore. She's always at Hank's. I can't blame her, but I feel bad."

"Do you want me to help you find a new place?"

"I'm afraid if I don't move soon I'm going to lose my daughter. Is it possible that we can get a house? I mean, buy one?"

Debbie knew Garnet's meagre income wouldn't allow him to qualify for much right now. He had only been there for about a month, and banks required gainful employment of a lot longer than that to consider someone for a mortgage. But, maybe it was possible to do something creative with him, like a rent-to-own contract?

"Let me think about it, Garnet, and I'll see what I can do. Listen, I'll see if I can talk to Carsdale today and I'll call you tonight, okay?"

"Susan probably won't be home tonight. And she's the only one with the phone right now."

She took his address and promised to stop by later.

After saying goodbye, she speed-dialed Brad.

"Listen, sorry about drunk-dialing you the other night."

"Hey, not a problem. Anyway, I always thought the most important thing about drunk-dialing is making the call. It's actually not important what you say, as long as you make the call."

Debbie chuckled in spite of herself. She couldn't deny the man made her smile. "I suppose so."

"You should start a course: How to Reach Your Financial Goals Through Drunk-Dialling."

Debbie laughed again. "Yeah, I'd be broke in a matter of months."

"Listen, I won't keep you, but I wanted to run a couple things by you, and I'd rather not do it over the phone. Can we meet for coffee sometime soon?"

"Is it business stuff? I have a pretty full slate today."

"Some business, some personal."

Debbie's curiosity was piqued. "Listen I have some running around to do today. Can you meet me at the usual spot at about three this afternoon?"

"I'll be there," he said.

Debbie finished most of her appointments before going to the hospital to talk to Cardsale.

She tracked him down in the hospital corridor and he led her to his office.

"Would you like some tea or coffee?" he asked.

"Tea would be nice. Black, if you have it."

He disappeared into the little kitchen adjoining his office and reappeared two minutes later with the hot beverages.

Debbie sipped her tea. She still felt out of sorts from the nightmare.

"As of today, Ella's EEG shows no brain activity. She's been in this coma for almost a month now, and her brain activity has slowly decreased over that period. And now, as I said, we have nothing. With zero brain activity, it appears unlikely she'll ever come out of this coma. And even if she did, she would exist in a vegetative state."

"Does Garnet know any of this yet?"

"I called him the other day and tried to prepare him as best I could. But, in his recovering condition, I'm not sure he fully understands the severity of the situation. He seemed to be in denial."

"He wasn't in denial this morning when I talked to him."

"Very well, then. But, since you're a good friend of the family, maybe you could help me get through to him."

"What do you want me to do?"

"I'm well aware that this is a moral dilemma for anyone. It's an ethical issue as well, to decide to play God, so to speak, and have to choose when a person's life should be ended. But, if she continues to deteriorate, it's an issue that needs addressing."

"What do you think we should do?"

"Well, since today is only the first day that shows absolutely no brain activity, we should wait a bit."

"How long?"

"That's ultimately up to Garnet and his daughter, but I'd say two weeks maximum. If she's the same as she is now in two weeks, the family should seriously consider taking her off life support."

Debbie was stunned. "I don't know what to say."

"You don't have to say anything. I'm just telling you how it is. And, if you could help me position this to Garnet as gently as possible, I would appreciate it."

"I'm sure there's another argument that could be made for keeping her alive."

"I've heard them all before. As I said, it's a moral dilemma that has been argued ad nauseam by much greater minds than my own. The argument to preserve life is rooted in religious doctrines and beliefs. And, yes, I'm a religious man, in case you were wondering."

Debbie wasn't sure how to handle this conundrum. She didn't want to encourage Garnet to pull the plug, and she didn't want any responsibility for Ella's death.

At the same time, she felt her fate was somehow intertwined with Ella's. Possibly because of the disturbing nightmares.

She knew Garnet was a religious man, and he would want to keep Ella alive as long as possible.

Carsdale cleared his throat. "Listen, I have to get back to work, but just think about what I said, and think about Ella, and how much longer would you want to make her suffer. As you know, she also has a brain tumour causing her a lot of distress, and could also hemorrhage at any time. The window to operate on it is closing."

Before leaving the hospital, Debbie went into Ella's room. She sat next to her and held her hand.

"I want you to come back to us, Ella. It's too early for you to go. Your family needs you. I need you. Please come back, Ella," she pleaded.

No eye movement.

No sign of recognition or understanding whatsoever

"Did I tell you I'm meeting Brad this afternoon for coffee? You know we've been friends for centuries, but my woman's intuition is telling me something different here. Oh, I could be completely wrong, but I think he's interested in me in another way. What do you think?"

No response.

"Listen, I have to go, sweetie, but I'll be back. Come back to us, please, Ella. We need you. I need you." She bent, kissed her friend on the cheek, and left.

Chapter Forty-Four

An hour later, she was sitting across from Brad. The conversation started with business,. Brad told her he was struggling to meet the deadline on a particular renovation he was doing for a client.

He wasn't dressed in business clothes today—it was paint-stained pants and a ripped, stained kangaroo jacket. He sported a two-day growth, but it accentuated his blue eyes and jet-black hair. He was in good shape, other than a slightly noticeable belly, the result of too many chicken wings and beer.

"Oh, you might have to work a little harder, but you'll make it," Debbie said, forcing herself to stay interested in shoptalk. She was thinking about Ella.

Finally Brad paused and stared at Debbie.

"Listen, I don't know how to say this," he said. "I've been starting to think of you differently lately, like someone I might want to have a relationship with. What do you think of that?"

Debbie had expected this. But with everything that had happened that day, she hadn't thought about how she was going to respond.

"I don't know, Brad. I'm not sure I'm ready for a relationship."

He looked at her, searching. "Do you think you could be interested in someone like me?"

Who was she trying to kid? Debbie had been doing Internet dating for the last three years. She had even tried speed-dating, and been set up by a few of her friends.

Deep down, she wanted a relationship.

She didn't know what to say.

"I don't know Brad. Listen, can we just be good friends, like we are right now, and leave that open for the time being? I have a lot of things on my plate, and I don't know that I can think about a relationship right now." She hoped that was good enough.

"No problem at all. Take as much time as you want. I'm not going anywhere. And I certainly don't want to ruin our friendship."

Chapter Forty-Five

Garnet tried to work. He kept getting distracted by domestic chores, and failed to produce a single note.

Early in the afternoon, his right hand had almost completely seized up and a massive headache developed, so Bud had let him go home early.

He looked at his keyboard. *Focus.* He started composing a few notes, then felt a sharp pain in his right hand. It wasn't doing what he wanted it to.

He turned the computer off and stared around the apartment. Pickles slept soundly on the couch.

He thought of calling Chaddie, but then realized he didn't have a phone. Susan had the only phone and she was spending the night at Hank's.

He was becoming more worried about his wife by the minute.

Ella was so much a part of his life he couldn't imagine not having her in it. He lay down on the bed, buried his head in the pillow, and cried. Then he stopped crying and did the only thing he could think of. He prayed. And prayed. And prayed some more.

The ceiling pounded. He could hear a conversation above. Drunk tenants, becoming drunker by the minute.

And louder.

Garnet's head still ached.

The ceiling thumped again. Then a large thud. "For fuck sakes," a voice upstairs said.

Garnet turned on his TV so he wouldn't have to hear the noise. The walls were paper-thin.

"Watch where you're walking," another voice said. A stereo was turned on. *At least the stereo was drowning out their words,* Garnet thought, so he wouldn't have to hear them swearing at each other.

He was about to cover his ears when the buzzer went. He was surprised he even heard it. "Hello?"

"Garnet, it's Debbie."

"Oh, come on up." He buzzed her in.

Debbie walked in the door, giving Garnet a quick hug and looking around the apartment. As usual, it was in a state of disarray.

Garnet was a lot of things, but a good housekeeper he was not.

Pickles, who had slept soundly through all the noise, was startled by the intrusion and leaped off the couch, retreating underneath it to hide.

"What's with all the noise?" Debbie asked, her voice barely audible.

"It's always like this."

"Can we go somewhere quieter?"

"Sure."

As they walked down the stairwell, a thunderous crash came from above.

They saw a fat, drunk and dishevelled man crumpled on the stairs, and a skinny man standing over him, kicking him repeatedly.

"You get the fuck outta here," Skinny said to Fatty. "You're a disrespectful son of a bitch."

Garnet thought better of stepping in. Debbie looked fearful.

The kicking continued. Fatty, crumpled in the stairwell, moaned in pain.

One of the blows dislodged him from his precarious perch, and he rolled down the stairs, coming to a crashing halt at the landing where Garnet and Debbie stood.

Debbie was already on her phone, dialling 911. "I'm calling the cops," she said.

A few of the other tenants heard the noises. Doors opened. People stared.

"Don't bother," an elderly woman said. "I already have."

Debbie clicked her phone off. Skinny stood a few steps above the crumpled man before him, surveying his handy work.

"Yer all a bunch a fuckin' rejects," he said, walking the few stairs up to his apartment. "Fuck you and fuck the cops," he added before retreating into his apartment and slamming the door.

Fatty must have weighed at least 250 pounds, and Debbie wasn't sure she could lift him. Garnet, with his post-stroke physical limitations, was in the same position.

Fatty lay on the floor, moaning and bleeding from his head, nose, and eye. Another door opened and a beefy biker came out. He helped Fatty to a seated position on the stairs. Debbie reached into her purse and offered him a packet of Kleenex tissue. The burly biker took it and winked at her.

He handed a few tissues to Fatty, who began wiping the blood from his wounds.

Debbie turned to the elderly lady. "Did you call an ambulance?"

"I did," she said. "This happens all the time."

Debbie looked horrified. "Let's get out of here," she said to Garnet.

About twenty minutes later they sat in a Ricky's restaurant.

Debbie sipped her tea and watched Garnet eat. He took a big bite of a burger, and some sauce dribbled down the right side of his face—the partially paralyzed side. He didn't realize it or didn't feel it, and kept chomping away at the burger.

She handed him a napkin. "You have some sauce on your face."

He set the half-eaten burger down, took the napkin, and wiped his chin.

"You got most of it, just a little bit on the other side."

He picked up another napkin and wiped the entire lower half of his face.

"I think you got it."

"Thanks," Garnet said.

Debbie talked while Garnet ate. "I have to get you out of that place. What a terrible environment. No wonder your daughter doesn't hang around there."

"If you could help, that would be great," Garnet said between bites.

"I'll see what I can come up with, Garnet. Let me think about it."

He nodded.

"Listen, I talked to Carsdale today. Have you heard from him?"

"He didn't call me at work. Maybe he called Susan, but I don't have a phone."

"Dr. Carsdale says as of today, there is no brain activity showing on the EEG."

Garnet stopped picking at his fries and looked up at Debbie. "Does that mean she's not going to come out of the coma?"

"They don't know that for sure. Let's just say that statistically, her chances don't look very good."

Garnet lost interest in his food and stared out the window. Finally, he said, "What do they want to do?"

"Carsdale says wait a few weeks and see what happens. But he wants you to at least start thinking about the possibility of taking her off life support."

Garnet didn't hesitate. "I can't do that. Regardless of how little the life force is, God has a plan in the whole scheme of things to preserve it. Nobody made me God, that I can decide when someone lives or dies. I won't take her off life support."

Debbie breathed a sigh of relief. *There, at least I've told him*, she thought, glad that Garnet, at least for now, wouldn't entertain the notion of pulling the plug on his wife.

Chapter Forty-Six

Earl sat at the fireplace with his back to her. Mona stood behind him. Ella, leaning in the doorway entrance, watched. Mona had finally agreed to talk to Earl.

"All right, I'll do it for my son."

Earl, startled, turned around. "Mona," he greeted her. "Do what for your son?"

"I'll forg ..."

Her words were drowned out by a loud roaring sound.

The demon smashed through the window, hovered, then landed on the floor in the middle of the three. His dark, muscular frame looked bigger than ever, his red eyes more menacing.

"You're all coming with me," he announced.

Ella backed up, fear gripping her.

Mona stiffened but did not react.

Earl rose from his chair. "You leave us be," he said. "You want me, you can have me, but you're not taking any of them."

"I want you all," the demon said. He turned to Mona. "Button your lips, young lady, and come with me. I assure you it will be an enjoyable journey."

"No," Ella screamed. "You leave us be."

Earl went for the shotgun, but the demon was quicker. He snatched it up and threw it out the broken window.

Earl stopped. Mona ran to him, took him in a passionate embrace, kissing him long and full on the lips. "I forgive you," she screamed. "I forgive you and I love you."

Earl knew it was time, but he hugged her tightly.

The demon frowned and flew up, circling the room, disappeared out the window.

A few seconds later, the apparition of Earl followed, sorrow and despair in his eyes. "Thank you, my love," he said to Mona. "You will always be in my heart."

And he disappeared as well.

Ella tiptoed around the glass, closing the wooden shutters, and the room was silent save for the crackling of the fire.

Mona crumpled to the floor.

Ella ran to her and knelt down. "I think you have a long journey ahead of you. Along with your son."

"Thanks so much for all your help," Mona said, tears streaming down her cheeks.

She slipped through Ella's grip in an instant and rose in the air. Charlie appeared in her arms and she cradled him, smiling.

"I will remember you," Mona said. "And I will watch over you." And then the two were gone, their images disappearing through the ceiling.

"I will remember you too," Ella said to an empty room.

She sat down in the chair by the fire and stared into it. Her mind raced with anticipation and excitement, hoping this was the end of her nightmare.

She hoped Mona and Charlie were now in a better place. As for Earl, well, she supposed he got what he deserved. At least in the afterlife, he showed some compassion.

Slowly, her mind went dark.

Chapter Forty-Seven

Two weeks later.

Garnet stared at his computer and forced himself to concentrate. He typed a few musical notes and paused to scribble a reminder of where "61 Titles" was going.

It was November early evening. Snow was falling.

Susan was at Hank's, where she had stayed twelve of the last fourteen nights.

Pickles slept comfortably on the couch, oblivious to the pounding music and argumentative voices coming from above.

Garnet removed his headphones, scratched his ear, and replaced them. The room became quiet again. He reviewed his work to date.

Each main title had three subtitles:

Fearfully And Wonderfully Made
Created In Him
Fear Unknown
Love

The Door Is Open
Journey
Your Heart's Desires
Fear No Evil

Open Road
Freedom Of The Wind

Passions
Revealed

Each title had accompanying music and his plan was to have the whole production acted out with dance, elaborate costumes, and a full orchestra, of which he would be a part—playing his trombone.

He had been practicing every day for the last two weeks, and he could feel it was starting to come back to him. He had even picked up one of his former piano students. Although Garnet couldn't play nearly the same as before, he was slowly regaining some marginal movement in his right hand.

He looked at the keyboard. Before he could move on to the next title, he had to finish composing the music for the subtitle, "Revealed."

He glanced around the room, ignoring the filthy mess, and refocused. His fingers moved along the keyboard, his right hand still unwilling to obey him on a few occasions.

He typed on in spite of the impediment, oblivious to everything but his work. He had poured himself into it over the course of the last two weeks. It was the only thing he could think of to take his mind off his problems.

He had been up to see his wife every single day for the past two weeks. On many visits, Debbie was also there. Garnet noticed a few times she reeked of alcohol, and he worried she had begun using it as a crutch.

There had been no change in Ella. Garnet had a meeting tomorrow to discuss options, which he knew meant only one thing: pulling the plug.

He had steadfastly refused to do this, but now his resolve was weakening. He was haunted by the thought that maybe he was making Ella suffer more than she had to. Carsdale had told him repeatedly that if she ever came out of the coma, her life in a vegetative state would be meaningless.

Susan had withdrawn from the emotional aspect of it, choosing to divert herself by spending all her time with her boyfriend. Garnet knew this was a coping mechanism for her.

He also knew why she wouldn't want to spend much time in his hellhole of an apartment.

Garnet composed music for about an hour and then noticed his phone, a recent addition to his life, flashing on the cluttered table beside him. It was ringing, but his headphones prevented him from hearing it.

He removed the headphones and answered it, fearing the worst.

"Garnet, how ya doin', man?" It was Chaddie. The two had become closer since finishing the course together. And, thanks to Garnet's encouragement, Chaddie had started a new job in construction.

"How are you?" Garnet asked.

"I rang the buzzer but you didn't answer. I'm downstairs."

"I'll open the door."

Chaddie walked in with a six-pack under one arm.

Pickles disappeared under the couch.

"Want one?" Chaddie asked, waving the six-pack in the air.

"No thanks."

Chaddie ignored the mess. "Looks like you've been busy."

"I'm trying to get my composition done."

"Am I interrupting?"

"No, I was just finishing up anyway."

Seated on the windowsill, Chaddie cracked a beer, lit a cigarette, took a long pull and exhaled out the open window. "Feel like goin' for a drive?"

"How many beers have you had?"

"This is my first. I'm good to go, honest."

"Where'd you have in mind?"

"Oh, I don't know, just a little cruise around town. We'll figure it out when we get there."

Garnet thought maybe a little fresh air would do him good. Besides, the noise upstairs was starting to drive him nuts.

"Neighbours getting a little unruly again, are they?"

"Every night it's the same."

"Want me to go up and have a friendly chat with them?"

"No, Chaddie. I have to live here."

"Your call. So, whadya say?"

"Sure, let's go."

Fifteen minutes later, Garnet was bundled up inside Chaddie's black pick-up.

Chaddie revved the motor, fishtailed out of his parking stall expertly, the wheels spinning on the icy pavement.

"I love this truck," he said, and laughed, a deep baritone sound.

Garnet chuckled, more at the sound of Chaddie's laugh than anything else.

Chapter Forty-Eight

Debbie hiccupped. The sound of it made her laugh, and she poured another glass of wine. She hiccupped again. She brought the full glass to her lips and drained half of it, hoping to cure her hiccups.

She waited a few minutes. No hiccups. "There, that's got it."

She sat in her outdoor hot tub by herself and drank. She had been there for well over an hour and was on her second bottle.

Since Brad's proposition, Ella's worsening condition, and Debbie's bitter realization that her life wasn't working, things had begun to unravel.

She did not know how to deal with the Brad situation. Since he had expressed his feelings, she had not returned a couple of his calls and was doing her best to ignore him. A few nights ago she had slipped up and drunk-dialled him again, and her recollection of what she said was vague at best.

She was drinking wine on a daily basis. She couldn't wait for her assistant to go home for the day so she could escape inside a bottle of white wine.

Or two.

She continued to have nightmares of Ella, demons, pig beasts, and haunted houses. Often, she would wake up petrified and drenched in sweat. And she didn't know why, but she remained haunted by these nightmares throughout the day.

More disturbing was the notion that she was connected to Ella's nightmare. And she wasn't sure that her concern for Ella was more of a selfish concern for her own well being.

She knew that the whole thing made no sense, and if she tried explaining it to anyone, they would think she was a lunatic.

Little by little, her business had begun to slip. Usually one to return calls at all hours of the night, now, when she wanted to retreat into her wine bottle, she would simply turn the phone off, drink, and wallow in self-pity.

And she was waking up later and later. That morning Lisa had arrived at eleven and had to wake Debbie so she could get some work done.

The tough executive veneer was beginning to crumble.

"To hell with it," she declared, draining the rest of her wine and refilling her glass. "I may be going to hell in a hand basket, but at least I'm enjoying the ride."

She was thinking about tomorrow. D-day. Garnet had to decide if he was going to pull the plug on his wife.

For no logical reason, Debbie worried that that would also spell her demise.

She took another sip of wine and thought of who she could call.

For all her beauty and success, no one came to mind.

Debbie knew hundreds of people who called her a friend. But, if push came to shove, would they be there for her?

She doubted it.

"Let me she, I mean see," she said aloud. A neighbour's dogged barked. "Brad, Ella, Garnet, Blake." Debbie drew a blank. She couldn't think of anyone else.

She picked up the phone and dialled Brad. Before he could pick up, she dropped the phone onto the snowy deck.

She took another sip of wine and slipped in the hot tub, her head plunging underwater. She brought her head up, coughing and sputtering, feeling around for the glass. Finally, she found it, emptied the water, and refilled it with wine.

The second bottle was empty.

"Time for a celebration," she said, stepping out of the hot tub in pursuit of a third bottle.

The deck leading into her kitchen was icy. She staggered, her right foot slipping out from under her. The momentum carried the second leg out, flinging her into the air.

She landed hard with a thud, her head the first point of contact on the icy deck. Blood sprayed onto the white, frozen deck.

Her world went black.

Brad was in the middle of a client renovation project when his phone rang. He picked it up, but the ringing had stopped.

He looked at the number and realized it was Debbie. He tried calling her back but it went straight to voicemail. He left a couple of messages.

And waited.

No response.

It was getting late. He was getting tired. And he was starting to worry. He tossed it over in his mind for about thirty minutes, and finally decided to go over to her house.

He stood outside her door, ringing her buzzer. Nothing. He tried calling her cell phone, then remembered he had her land line in his contact list.

He flipped to it and dialled the landline. Four rings and then to voicemail. He didn't leave a message.

He decided to look around the house. He walked into the backyard, and to his horror discovered Debbie splayed out on the back deck, a pool of blood oozing from her head, forming a growing red circle in the snow.

He felt for a pulse. She had one. He breathed a sigh of relief and called 911.

The pool of blood around her was already partially frozen, and he calculated she had been unconscious for at least two hours.

The 911 operator had told him not to move her, in spite of the frigid temperatures, but he decided to make an executive decision. He was worried about her freezing to death.

He pulled open the sliding glass door to her kitchen, went in the house, and retrieved a large sleeping bag from one of her closets. He rolled her onto the sleeping bag, and pulled it through the sliding doors and into the kitchen. She was losing a lot of blood, and the yellow sleeping bag quickly became stained a dark red.

He then went into the backyard, turned off the hot tub, cleaned up the fragments of a broken wine glass, and found her phone buried in the snow.

He re-entered the house, put the cell phone on the table to dry, kneeled down beside her and waited. She reeked of alcohol.

"Don't die on me," he said. "Hang in there. Please."

Moments later, paramedics arrived and began working on Debbie. "Did you move her?" one of them asked Brad.

"Yes, it's cold out and I was worried about her freezing."

"What happened?"

"Looks to me like she fell getting out of the hot tub."

"Probably drunk," the paramedic said. He glanced at the hot tub and noticed the empty wine bottles.

A few minutes later, they loaded her into a waiting ambulance.

"Where you taking her?" Brad asked.

"Foothills," the man said, closing the ambulance doors and speeding away.

Brad locked up Debbie's house, started his car, and drove to the hospital.

Four hours later he was still in the waiting room, drinking coffee and pacing.

Finally Dr. Carsdale walked into the room.

"How is she?"

"She's stable. She cracked her skull during the fall, and was knocked unconscious. She came back around just before we ran the EEG."

"And?"

"She's confused. She suffered a nasty concussion, and we want to monitor her for a few days, make sure she doesn't slip into a coma, try and determine the extent of the damage. It looks like the concussion was the only injury, but we want to be sure."

"So she's going to be okay?"

"It looks like it, yes, but with head concussions we can never be too sure. There is so much about them we don't understand."

Brad breathed a sigh of relief. "Can I see her?"

"I don't think that's such a good idea right now. It's late, she's still pretty disoriented, and she needs to rest. Why don't you go home, get some sleep, and come back tomorrow."

"Sounds like a good idea," Brad said, tossing his empty Styrofoam cup into the wastebasket.

"One more thing," Carsdale said as Brad began walking away. "She's lucky to be alive. She lost a lot of blood, and if you hadn't rescued her she would have died. You did a great job."

"Thanks," Brad said.

"What is it with these people?" Carsdale asked as Brad opened the door to leave.

"Excuse me?"

"First Garnet has a stroke during brain surgery, then Ella falls down some stairs, suffers a concussion, and slips into a coma, and now her friend Debbie falls and suffers a concussion. I sure hope this is the end of it all."

"Me too," Brad said.

Chapter Forty-Nine

Garnet sat on the bus, staring out the window at the falling snow. Susan sat beside him. The two did not speak. They were going to meet with Carsdale and determine Ella's fate.

Garnet was tired and strung out. Chaddie's visit last night had provided a momentary diversion. The two had driven around downtown for a while, and finally Chaddie parked in Glenmore Park, where they looked at the frozen reservoir and talked.

Garnet had heard very little of what his friend said. He was suffering from anticipatory dread.

On the way home, he had the urge to call Debbie, but then realized it was far too late and he had forgotten his cell phone.

Susan snapped him out of his recollections. "Are you going to pull the plug on Mom?"

"I don't think so, honey."

"You don't think so. You mean you're not sure."

"I'm confused about the whole thing. What do you want me to do?" He looked at her and she turned her head away from his gaze.

Finally she turned around and stared directly into his eyes. "I think we should let God decide. And we're not God."

"Listen, whatever happens, we'll make the decision together. I promise you that. And we both have to agree on it."

Susan gave a small smile.

He looked at her and did his best to muster a smile. They fell silent again, preoccupied with their own thoughts.

Garnet closed his eyes and prayed.

Susan and Garnet arrived at the hospital and went directly into Carsdale's office. He brought them up to speed on Ella's condition—no change—and also told them Debbie now shared a room with Ella, the result of a fall and subsequent concussion.

Garnet's jaw dropped open. "What next?" he asked.

"With no brain activity, your wife is technically living life in a vegetative state right now," he explained. "You have to think about her quality of life, whether you want her to live in this condition, and for how long."

"Is there any chance at all she could come out of it normal?" Garnet asked.

"Yes, there is, but it is very small. The numbers are similar to your chances of winning the lottery. Did you know you have a better chance statistically of getting struck by lightning four times than you do of winning the lottery?"

Garnet didn't like Ella's chances.

"It would take nothing short of a miracle for her to come out of this and be able to lead a normal life."

A miracle is exactly what Garnet had prayed for.

"I would like to think about it," he said. "I need some time."

The room shared by the two patients was crowded with visitors: Janice Priestly, Carsdale, Brad, Lisa, Garnet, and Susan.

Janice adjusted Ella's monitors. Carsdale stood beside Debbie's bed, chart in hand. The privacy curtain had been pulled back so Debbie had a view of her friend. She was awake but disoriented. A white bandage was wrapped around her head. The faces in front of her slowly came into focus.

"Where am I," she said. "Who are you?"

"I'm Dr. Carsdale. Do you remember me?"

A recollection of events and people came to her. "Uhh, yeah, I think so."

Debbie looked over at Ella, searched the other faces, and tried to smile when she recognized them.

"Listen, I'll let you visit with your friends," Carsdale said. "I just wanted to tell you we'll be keeping you here for a few days to monitor you. We also want to do another EEG to try and determine the exact severity of your concussion. You should not be working for at least the next two months."

"What? I have to work," Debbie said.

"Your health is far more important." Carsdale asked her a series of questions relating to cognitive ability, made some notes on his chart, and left.

It was Brad who spoke first. "How are you, Debbie?"

"I'm a little dizzy right now."

"Listen, I found your phone after I found you and gave it to Lisa."

Lisa smiled and waved it in the air. "It works, Debbie. I blow-dried it."

"Found me?" Debbie asked. She still could not recall the circumstances that had brought her here.

"You took a little fall—well, a big fall—getting out of your hot tub. It's a good thing you called me just before you fell, otherwise we might not be having this conversation."

"Thank you," Debbie said, her memory of the events becoming clearer.

"No problem. Listen, if there's anything you need, don't hesitate to call me."

"Thanks again."

Brad was exhausted.

"Listen, I'm going to go. I'm glad you're okay. Call me if you need anything at all, okay?"

"Thanks, sweetie. I owe you one."

"You don't owe me anything," Brad said.

Garnet sat down beside Ella. He looked at his wife, then at Debbie. "I'm so glad you're okay," he said. "I just found out."

Debbie looked at him blankly, the full realization of her predicament beginning to sink in.

Lisa waited patiently for her boss to give her the day's tasks.

Susan whispered into her mother's ear.

"If you need anything at all, you let me know, okay?" Garnet said.

"Thanks," Debbie said, wondering if in the days to come her other "friends" would visit her. She looked over at Ella, motionless. Susan felt the eyes on her and smiled at Debbie.

"What's happening with Ella?" Debbie asked.

Ella was in a dark place. She had left the Fantasma Retreat Centre, only to be stuck in a black abyss. She could hear the voices around her speaking. And, in her mind, she could respond to them. But they couldn't hear her words. She tried again. "I'm here, please don't let me die like this. Help me."

"We need you to come back to us," Susan whispered into her mother's ear. "We need you, Mom. Come back, please."

"I'm here honey, I'm here. I want to come back."

Susan bent down and kissed Ella on the cheek.

Ella could feel it, knew it was her daughter, and tried to reach out and touch her. Her arms would not move.

She screamed, "I'm here, I'm here, I don't want to die. Please, please don't let me die."

"I can't do it," Garnet said to Debbie. "There's still no brain activity, but I just can't do it."

Debbie was relieved. "You have to follow the dictates of your heart, Garnet."

Garnet also tried talking to his wife, but to no avail. So they left.

Even Debbie, in her condition, had spoken a few words to her friend.

But Ella would not respond.

Debbie, after delegating business tasks to Lisa, sat alone with her thoughts, a comatose Ella beside her. She watched Ella's steady breathing and wondered how she could possibly help her.

She could use a drink.

Soon, the medication took effect and she drifted off.

Chapter Fifty

Debbie wandered through a dark tunnel, feeling her way around. It smelled damp and musty. She pinched herself, wondering if she was dreaming or had slipped into a coma, like her friend.

She heard a snarling sound. She jerked her head around and saw two glowing eyes behind her. She struggled to make out the features. Beast-like creatures with pig heads.

They snarled and slowly walked toward her.

Awfully pig-headed, she thought, and picked up her pace. The snarling grew louder. She looked behind her again. They were gaining on her. Now she was afraid, and she felt her body tense up. *Run*. But her legs would not obey. The best she could do was a fast walk.

Then her legs did respond, and she ran in complete blackness, stumbling and falling a few times, picking herself up, and continuing her escape. She rounded a corner. She saw a light in the distance and a small widening of the tunnel. It lit her way and she continued, now panting for breath, raw fear coursing through her body.

She arrived at the small opening, stopped, and searched around for a place to hide.

She saw a small hole and crawled in it.

She touched something warm. Her eyes adjusted to the light.

It was Ella. Curled up in a fetal position.

She appeared to be sleeping.

"Ella, Ella, wake up," Debbie yelled. She curled around her friend's body and whispered in her ear. "Wake up, please. It's time to go."

Ella slowly opened her eyes. Blinking in disbelief, she said, "Debbie, it's you."

Then fear darkened her face. "The pig beasts, where are they?"

"They're coming. Listen." The two hugged each other as the growls and footsteps neared.

They tensed, listening. Game over.

But then the sounds faded into the distance.

They remained silent until all they could hear was their own beating hearts and breathing. "Let's go," Debbie said. "They passed us. Let's go the other way."

She helped Ella to her feet and the two began walking down the dark tunnel in the opposite direction.

They heard a loud whooshing sound and were suddenly swept off their feet by a tidal wave. The torrent carried them down the winding tunnel, and they clung to each other for safety. Their heads submerged under water, and they popped up again, coughing for air.

Debbie saw an opening where the water was draining out. It looked like a waterfall, and they were heading toward it, travelling much too fast to do anything about it.

They were helpless.

She hugged Ella tighter and closed her eyes.

In an instant, they arrived at the opening, and were flung out with the water, still clinging to one another.

They were falling fast. Debbie looked down. All she could see was an outcrop of jagged boulders.

They looked at each other and screamed.

Ella forced herself to look down again and saw the rocks below growing bigger.

Seconds before they smashed onto the rocks, Ella opened her eyes.

Debbie was clinging to her, screaming loudly. She looked around and registered the hospital room.

She feared her friend would hit the bottom, never wake up. "Wake up, Debbie, wake up," she said and shook her violently.

Debbie's eyes suddenly opened, and she looked at her friend in disbelief.

She was in Ella's bed, wrapped in a tight embrace.

"Ella, it's you, you're alive."

"Yes, and so are you."

"Thank God."

"You can say that again."

"Thank God."

The two laughed and hugged.

"We have to stop meeting like this," Debbie said.

As she got out of the bed, she noticed her friend's expression change. Ella's eyes rolled back into her head, and she began convulsing violently.

"Oh shit," Debbie said, staggering toward the panic button. She started yelling, "Help, help, help," and pressed the button.

Ella rocked back and forth in her bed.

In a minute, Janice was in the room. She quickly examined Ella and was back in an instant with a team of medical staff.

Debbie sat on her bed, worried and confused, watching the staff swarm around Ella.

"Let's get her in the OR," Carsdale said. "I think her brain tumour is hemorrhaging."

Ella was loaded onto a stretcher and whisked away.

Chapter Fifty-One

It was mid-afternoon the following day, and Garnet was at his post—shining shoes. And worrying about Ella. He hadn't slept more than an hour the previous night, and the little sleep he did have was permeated by a nightmare that involved screams, snarls, and rushing water. He vaguely remembered seeing his wife, but now he wasn't sure. His memory of the nightmare had faded as soon as he bolted upright in his bed, eyes wide open.

After that, he was not able to go back to sleep, so he had tossed and turned and fretted.

He adjusted his right arm to hold his shoeshine rag, bringing his mind back into the present.

The phone rang. Bud picked it up. "It's for you, and it's urgent."

Garnet dropped his rag and limped over to the phone. "I'll be right back, sir," he said to his customer. "I'm sorry."

"Hello."

"Garnet, it's Dr. Carsdale."

"Hi," he said, fear in his voice.

"Are you sitting down?"

Garnet plopped down in an unoccupied barber chair. "I am now. What's up?"

"I have some good news and some bad news."

A long pause. Garnet held his breath and braced himself for the worst.

"The good news is Ella came out of her coma last night. The bad news is she woke up in shock and it caused a massive hemorrhage in her brain tumour."

Garnet was stunned. He tried to speak but no words would come.

"Are you there?" Dr. Carsdale asked.

"Yes, I'm here."

"Okay. We operated last night. It was a twelve-hour operation, and I just finished now. It looks like we were able to stem the hemorrhage. Ultimately, time will tell, so we'll have to see. I didn't want to operate right away, but we had no choice. It was an emergency, and we had to act fast."

"Did you remove the tumour?"

"Yes, it looks like we got all of it."

"How is she?"

"She's still under anesthetic, so we'll have to wait and see. But she came out of the coma, and, according to Debbie, who was with her when she woke up, she appeared to have normal brain function. They had a brief conversation before the tumour hemorrhaged."

Garnet breathed a sigh of relief. "What, exactly, was the bad news again?"

"The bad news is that because, in terms of health, she wasn't an ideal candidate for surgery, we're not sure how she will recover from this and what, if any, brain damage may have resulted."

Bud busied himself finishing the shoes of Garnet's customer, as the man was showing signs of impatience.

"When can I see her?"

"It's not a good idea to come tonight. She's still under and while she should be coming around soon, she's going to be very groggy and in a lot of pain. Listen, I have to get back to work. I'll have Janice call you when she wakes up, okay? She's working the nightshift tonight."

"Okay," Garnet said, returning to his customer.

"It's okay, Garnet," Bud said. "I'll handle it. Why don't you take fifteen minutes, go and get yourself a pop or something."

Garnet nodded, grabbed his cell phone and jacket, and walked out into the blistering cold. He had to call Susan and give her an update.

Chapter Fifty-Two

Debbie slept. She had been hauled off earlier for another EEG, and Carsdale had notified her that it appeared Ella's operation was a success.

Before she had dozed off, Dr. Carsdale had reiterated that she must not attempt to work too hard for the next couple of months. Some delegating was permissible, but he did not want her seeing clients or spending the whole day in the office. She needed rest, and he wanted her in the hospital for a few more weeks.

Accustomed to always being on the run, Debbie hadn't taken the news particularly well. She was also saddened by the fact she had not had a single visitor.

Of all the friends she thought she had, no one was there. *Am I really that much of a bitch?*

She blinked and her world slowly came into focus. The first thing she saw was red. As her vision cleared, she realized it was large bouquet of roses. Behind it, Brad's smiling face.

"How are you?"

"Uh ..." she wiped her eyes. "Had a long night. Ella came out of her coma." She gestured to the empty bed next to her and explained what had happened.

"What are these?" she asked.

"They're roses," Brad responded, smiling.

"For me?"

"Do you see anyone else in the room?"

"Thanks, that's an awfully nice gesture."

"No problem, least I could do for my good friend."

Debbie glanced at the empty bed beside her. "Where's Ella?" she asked.

"You just told me she had an operation last night, and she's still under."

"Oh, right. I did, didn't I?"

Since the concussion, Debbie had serious doubts about the power of her short-term memory. "Don't worry," Brad said, "it'll come back to you. It's normal after a concussion that your mind won't be able to process information the same way. Your brain is bruised. It's healing."

She was surprised at his insight. "You've had a concussion before?"

"When I was a kid, I fell off a roof doing construction and cracked the side of my skull. I didn't feel the same for a long time."

"And you eventually fully recovered?"

"I think so, but I've never been given credit for having a lot of intelligence, so who knows. I can lift heavy things though, so I guess I'm good for something."

Debbie smiled. "What time is it?" she asked.

"It's six thirty-five. You expecting someone? Cause if you are, I can leave."

"No, I was just wondering what time Ella might be coming back. I'm worried."

"I'm sure she'll be fine."

Debbie looked at the roses again. "They're beautiful, Brad. Did I thank you?"

"Yes, you did."

"Oh." A food services employee entered and deposited a tray of food in front of her. She picked at the mashed potatoes and meatloaf.

"Would you like me to leave while you eat? Or can I get you anything?"

"No and no," Debbie said, pushing a spoonful of mashed potatoes into her mouth. She glanced at the bed again. "What time is it?"

"It's six forty," Brad said gently.

After a half hour visit, Brad left.

Debbie was just finishing her dinner when Ella was wheeled back into the room.

"Is she conscious?" she asked Janice.

"Oh yes, she's conscious, all right. Groggy, but conscious. If you can help it, I would try not to talk to her too much, she's going to be really dozy and awfully tired. I'd be surprised if she stays awake for longer than an hour."

"No problem," Debbie said.

Janice and a porter positioned Ella in the bed, adjusted some pillows, taking care to elevate her head and right leg, which was still in a cast from her fall over a month ago. Janice hooked up some monitors and checked her IV. Then she stood over Ella's bed, smiling,

"How proud I am of my patient," she said as Ella groggily acknowledged her praise.

Ella glanced at Debbie and smiled. Debbie returned it.

When the nurse and porter had left, Debbie waited a few minutes before asking, "How are you, honey?"

"I'm glad to …" She trailed off, coughing. She cleared her throat and continued, "… to be among the living."

Debbie was overjoyed. Tears of happiness streamed down her cheeks. She couldn't remember ever being so happy in her entire life. She pulled a napkin off the food tray and wiped away her tears.

"I'm going to let you rest. We have a lifetime to talk."

Chapter Fifty-Three

Six weeks later.

"Where are you taking us?" Garnet asked.

"It's a surprise," Debbie responded matter-of-factly.

"Okay," he said. Garnet and Ella became quiet with anticipation, sitting comfortably in the back seat, holding hands and staring dreamily into each other's eyes. Like newlyweds.

Debbie sat in the front seat with Don as he expertly weaved through rush-hour traffic and into Falconridge, a multi-ethnic, northeast community that had good access to schools, shopping, and main arteries.

Falconridge wasn't an upscale area by any standard, but it wasn't a ghetto. It was dotted with predominantly 1980's homes, and the city had just announced it would be extending the northeast leg of the light-rail transit out there soon, making the downtown commute for residents much easier in the years to come.

Debbie's recovery from the concussion had been a lot quicker than any of the doctors had expected. Although she was going against doctor's orders, she had decided this one tour of duty would be worth the risk.

Since her release from hospital, Debbie had re-evaluated her whole life, laid off one of her assistants, and reduced her other assistant to part-time. After coming so close to death, money no longer intrigued her like it had before.

On the precipice of becoming a self-destructive alcoholic, the downtime gave her a lot of time for reflection. She planned on selling her posh mansion to reduce her overhead, and to devote more of her life to what mattered, helping other people achieve their dreams.

She had no idea how she was going to accomplish this yet. After all, she was still on the mend. But she had definitely turned a corner in her thinking.

She had even started to re-evaluate her earlier pessimistic view of Brad, and she found the two were growing closer, with the possibility of a romantic connection in the near future.

She found that in her time of need, the friends she thought she had were nowhere to be found.

On the other hand, Brad was always there for her when she needed him. Recently, he had asked her out on a date and she had accepted. Brad promised to entertain her at his modest two-bedroom condo and whip up one of his culinary wonders.

The nightmares had ceased for both Debbie and Ella, and they no longer talked about the dark places they had been together, or the dark place Ella had visited during her coma.

Ella thought she could, at times, feel Mona's presence, but she dared not speak about it to anyone. She had decided not to tell her husband or daughter about the experience and, along with Debbie, made a vow of secrecy.

Ella had been released from the hospital earlier that day. Debbie made sure she was there to pick her up. In her days in the hospital, Ella and Debbie had gotten quite close, often staying up until the wee hours of the morning to talk.

According to Carsdale, Ella had suffered some brain damage as a result of the hemorrhage. While she already had issues with short-term memory and processing information, now it seemed her long-term memory was also affected. Only time would tell how much her brain would be able to recover from the trauma.

Garnet, in between shoe shining, had been focused on the development of his musical career. He had finished "61 Titles," and had submitted it, along with other pre-requisite material, to Berklee College of Music. He had also taken up the piano again, making a point of practicing at his church every chance he got.

The right side of his face was still contorted, he still limped, and his right hand often gave him trouble.

But he believed, contrary to the opinions of his medical practitioners, he would one day regain full use of his facial, hand, and leg muscles.

He also believed beyond a doubt he would not only be accepted to Berklee with a full scholarship, but he would graduate one day and go on to become a successful composer and music teacher.

With Garnet's influence, Chaddie had also become a different person. He had not given up alcohol entirely, but Garnet had noticed his consumption had decreased dramatically.

Garnet wondered what Debbie had up her sleeve as the Lexus turned into the driveway of the small green bungalow.

"We're here," Debbie announced.

They got out of the car and walked up on the front porch. Debbie stopped and searched her purse.

Garnet realized that Debbie hadn't talked on the phone to clients once during the entire trip.

"Where's your phone?" he asked, surprised by the change.

"Oh, I don't do that anymore, Garnet," she said, smiling and putting her arm around him. "Not only is it rude and disrespectful to the people I'm with," Debbie said. "But doctor's orders are that I shouldn't be overworking my little brain. But, don't worry, I've turned a corner." She put her arm around Ella. "I now have some perspective on what really matters in life."

She pulled out a key and opened the front door.

Susan sat on the couch smiling cheerfully, while Pickles dozed on her lap peacefully.

"That reminds me," Debbie said. "Thank you both for helping me and for being so important to my newfound happiness. I love you guys." She hugged them both.

"Now, come in and see your new place. Welcome home!"

Also by William Blackwell

Phantom Rage, Poison Rage, Infected Rage
Nightmare's Edge
Resurrection Point
Brainstorm
Rule 14
Assaulted Souls
Assaulted Souls II
Assaulted Souls III
Blood Curse
Black Dawn
The Strap
The End is Nigh
Orgon Conclusion
Freaky Franky
The Witch's Tombstone
The Dark Menace
Tales of Damnation
In Your Dreams
Macabre Alley

Freaky Franky Preview

"If you're looking for a horror with a slice of religion, I recommend this book. It's one of the greatest horror novels I've ever read and it's not a cliché plot. I rate this book 10/10." Goodreads

"If you love a good tense novel with deep moral undertones then this one's for you!" -Amazon

When an enigmatic town doctor saves the life of Anisa Worthington's dying son, she abandons Christianity in favor of devotion to the cult of Saint Death. Some believe the mysterious skeleton saint will protect their loved ones; help in matters of the heart; provide abundant happiness, health, wealth and justice.

But others, including the Catholic Church, call it blasphemous, evil and satanic.

Anisa introduces Saint Death to troubled Catholic friend Helen Randon and strange things begin happening. One of Helen's enemies is brutally murdered and residents of Montague, a peaceful little town in Prince Edward Island, begin plotting to rid the Bible belt of apostates.

Anisa suspects Helen is perverting the good tenets of Saint Death but, before she can act, a terrible nightmare propels her to the Dominican Republic in search of Freaky Franky, her long-lost and unstable brother, who mysteriously disappeared without a trace twenty years ago.

To her horror, Anisa learns Freaky Franky is also worshiping Saint Death with evil intentions. As a fanatical and hell-bent lynch mob tightens the noose, mysterious murders begin occurring all around Anisa. Unsure about who's an enemy and who's an ally, she's thrust into a violent battle to save her life as well as the lives of her unpredictable friends and brother.

About the Author

Canadian dark fiction author William Blackwell studied journalism at Mount Royal University and English literature at The University of British Columbia. He worked as a journalist for many years before pursuing his passion for storytelling. His novels have been characterized as graphic, edgy, and at times terrifying. Currently living on a secluded acreage on Prince Edward Island, Blackwell finds much of his inspiration from Mother Nature, odd people, traveling, and bizarre nightmares.

Author Comments

Thank you for reading this book. I would be eternally grateful if you would post a book review on your favorite book retailer website. A positive review is the highest compliment a writer can receive. Reviews are crucial to the success of any author and help readers discover new books. You don't have to say much. A few sentences will suffice.

In other news, I have a gift for you. Complete the signup form contained in the link below with your name and email address and download a FREE copy of *Resurrection Point*, a dark tale about the horrifying consequences of experimenting with death and resurrection. You'll be kept up to date on blog posts, new releases, and freebies. I promise I won't spam you and you can unsubscribe at any time.

Thanks again for your support.

http://www.wblackwell.com/free-ebook/